FIRSTBORN ACADEMY

SHADOW WITCH

ISLA FROST

Published by JFP Trust
2019 First Digital Edition

ISBN: 9780 6482532 7 3

www.islafrost.com

CHAPTER ONE

My mind was still my own when I woke.

Theus hadn't lied then. The transformation ritual did not change who we were. Only our magic. And according to Lirielle, my wildcard gift would shake the worlds.

But my immediate concerns were much smaller. Relief that I'd survived washed through me, followed immediately by the overwhelming need to see my friends. To know that they too were okay.

Actually, *seeing* anything would be a good start. Wherever I was—probably the creepy transformation chamber if I had to guess—was as black as the gullet of a shadow stalker.

Whatever my new powers might be, they apparently didn't include enhanced night vision.

"Hello?" I couldn't hear anyone in the chamber with me, but you never knew with world walkers.

No answer.

"Millicent?" I asked.

There was still no answer because I was talking to a building—or a manor as she preferred to be called. But Millicent was sentient and understood me just fine.

"Um, would you mind opening the wall?"

Light cracked into the room, painfully bright. My eyelids weren't thick enough, so I flung an arm over my face as well.

While I waited for the light to stop hurting, I assessed what sort of shape I was in. We'd been told we would wake up weak, that we'd require bed rest. Yet the only way I felt different was, well, *better*.

I felt oddly energized. Bouncy even. Rather than as if my blood had been drained out, filtered through the body of one of the beings that had destroyed most of the human race, and put back in again.

Huh.

As soon as I could open my eyes without them watering, I sat up and swung my legs over the side of the narrow bed.

That was when I saw the woman's body.

CHAPTER TWO

My fingers were on the woman's throat, searching for a pulse before I realized that world walkers might not have an artery there. I'd seen them bleed. At least I'd seen *one* of them bleed. So they probably had a pulse. But I detected no fluttering heartbeat beneath my fingers. And the skin I touched was cold.

I angled my ear to hover above her nose and mouth, trying to feel the tickle of breath or hear even the barest whisper of shifting air.

Nothing.

I rocked back on my knees. Who was she? What had happened to her?

The stranger was strikingly attractive. Most world walkers were. The old stories had it wrong. Monsters were not gruesome misshapen things that repelled you on sight. They were arresting, bewitching, more beautiful versions of ourselves who possessed the power to destroy the world and had zero compunctions about doing it.

Humankind had learned that lesson at the cost of most of the earth's population. We should have shot first, should never have indulged our curiosity or the desire to feast our eyes upon their splendor. But the realization came too late.

This walker's strong but elegant features would have befitted the beloved warrior queen of some war-torn kingdom. Her face somehow still fierce and compelling even as she lay motionless and vulnerable in the dirt.

I was troubled by her death—if that's what it was. Not so much for her sake as for what it might mean. Theus had said the transformation ritual was dangerous for walkers too, but I hadn't really believed him. Hadn't thought he'd meant the lethal sort of danger.

Now I was forced to reassess. And it made what I'd been told about the Firstborn Academy's purpose even more nonsensical. Why on earth would the walkers go to such great lengths—the Agreement, the academy, and the transformation ritual that apparently risked their own lives—just to acquire a few humans with above-average magic?

They'd revealed a few days ago that we would be trained alongside the walker students to become a specialized contingent of elite warriors. They had *not* revealed who we were being trained to fight against.

I couldn't imagine an enemy that would warrant such efforts by the incredibly powerful world walkers.

More pressingly, what did *this* walker's death mean for me? Would they blame me for it? Had the ritual been completed, or was I still *just* me?

Maybe that was why I felt good. Great even. Like I'd woken up from an especially invigorating nap. Her death might have had nothing to do with the ritual. Perhaps she'd simply keeled over and died from whatever walkers die of, like clogged arteries or something, before she could begin.

I snorted at my overly optimistic train of thought. Unlikely.

Still, they couldn't blame me for her death, could they? They were the ones who'd forced the ritual upon me. I'd had no choice in the matter. The fact I'd gone willingly, hoping to gain a power that might help overthrow them, was irrelevant.

I knew it was callous to find a stranger dead at my feet and think only of the repercussions to myself. But she was a walker. They were responsible—directly and indirectly—for the deaths of billions of humans.

Except Ameline's question echoed in my head. Was *this* walker responsible?

I looked her over again. She seemed too young. If she was human, I'd guess she was in her thirties, but walkers aged differently, so she might have been significantly older. Old enough to have been there fifty years ago.

Even so, my attention fell on her luminous dark eyes that stared unseeing at the ceiling, this horrid cell the last thing she would ever see. And I found myself wondering about her family, her loved ones. A foolish way to think for someone who was hell-bent on taking them down.

Kneeling beside her body, I realized in all my secret scheming to overthrow the walkers, I'd never envisaged the dead I might leave in my wake.

I stood up, unwilling to pursue that train of thought any further. If the woman at my feet was truly dead—and I had a sick certainty that she was—then there was nothing I could do. And her stillness, her sightless dark eyes, fueled my need to escape from this creepy cell and find Ameline. Find Bryn.

So I left the stranger lying there on the dirt floor of the chamber and fled. Out of Millicent's basement. Along the first-floor corridor. Toward the dorm room I'd shared with my friends for the past three months.

Except I didn't make it.

"What's going on?" Professor Grimwort accosted me in the corridor. "How are you walking without assistance? Where's Kyrrha?"

"Um, I don't—"

Without waiting for an explanation (admittedly I didn't have a good one anyway), Grimwort seized my arm in an iron grip and dragged me back the way I'd come.

"You will accompany me until I get to the bottom of this."

"I need to see my friends," I protested.

He shot me a glare that might've shriveled the insides of a lesser mortal. His deep-set blue eyes were always shadowed and often contemptuous, and combined with his tall, angular build, the professor had excellent glaring capabilities.

"And I need to see mine," he said. "Why isn't Kyrrha with you? What happened during your ritual?"

I swallowed. "I don't know. She was like that when I woke up—"

"Like what?"

But I didn't need to answer, because he could now see for himself.

The woman's body, lying there where I'd left her.

Grimwort drew in a sharp breath. And when he spoke again, his voice was laden with command and tightly leashed fury.

"Sit. Down."

He jabbed a finger at a corner of the basement without taking his eyes off the body.

I sat.

Within a few minutes, three other professors had joined Grimwort. Each one followed the same pattern of behavior. They would look at the dead woman, blanch or show some other sign of shock, then turn to stare at me.

The most disconcerting thing was not the stares themselves but the emotion behind them.

Fear.

Except for Professor Cricklewood. In his eyes? I'd read speculation.

Neither reaction made any sense to me.

And now the professors were muttering among themselves. Too quiet for me to hear, except one word that was repeated enough times that I eventually made it out: Malus. The name the walkers had given the monstrous, devouring darkness they'd brought with them that had wiped out life from Europe and beyond.

But the Malus hadn't made it to our continent. Not yet. So that made no sense either. Did they think the monster had somehow crossed thousands of miles to kill this woman in the middle of my transformation ritual?

I was growing increasingly ill at ease. What the hell was going on?

The professors murmured some more, the conversation seeming to grow contentious yet no louder than before. Not loud enough to overhear.

If they hadn't been throwing frequent glances in my direction, I might have tried sneaking out.

I should have tried anyway.

Grimwort stalked over to me and grabbed my arm again. "Come with me."

His eyes were hard and wet, and every one of my instincts screamed that following him was a bad idea.

But refusing him was probably worse. So I cooperated.

He towed me to one of the tower rooms that spanned the full height of the manor. It was the room I'd arrived in when I'd stepped through the runegate all those months ago. A single window high above allowed cold winter light to shine down on the threadbare rug that covered the ancient timber floor. Aside from the rug, the only furnishings were an antique writing desk and a high-backed timber chair upholstered in faded velvet. No fireplace, no wall lamps, and no decoration but for the eccentric wallpaper that graced almost every one of Millicent's rooms.

It was still more pleasant than the basement.

Professor Grimwort shoved me through the doorway and spoke in a voice rough with grief.

"Millicent, do *not* let Nova out of this room under any circumstances until I say otherwise. Do I make myself clear? Disobey me in this and we'll strip you of sentience so fast you won't be able to twitch a floorboard, then burn you to the ground out of spite."

He wheeled and left, slamming the door behind him with enough force to rattle.

CHAPTER THREE

The door vanished, becoming just another part of the wall. Millicent did things like that. And after the threat Grimwort had thrown her way, I couldn't blame her.

I paced the sparsely furnished room. I needed to see my friends, dammit. And instead they'd shut me in here without explanation.

I was confused. I was frustrated. I was famished. Worst of all, I was starting to feel scared.

Grimwort had never paid me any special attention, never given any human student more than the bare minimum of his notice that I'd seen. He acted as if we were beneath him, as if we were wasting his time. But his dislike was impersonal.

At least it had been.

That had changed from the moment he'd seen his friend Kyrrha on the floor. Now he *noticed* me, all right. And I didn't like it one bit.

What on earth was going on? What were they planning on doing with me?

Hours passed without answer.

I paced. I sat. I contemplated attempting to escape, then concluded I couldn't do that to Millicent.

She'd survived hundreds of years of human industry and then the end of our world. Who was I to bring about her downfall? Besides, after a rough start, we'd become friends of sorts.

In the window high above, the sky grew dark.

And with no interior lamps for Millicent to adjust, the room grew dark too.

The need to know whether my friends were all right was a physical ache in my chest.

At least the dark I could do something about.

When we'd first arrived, Ameline, Bryn, and I had explored every inch of this room, searching for an escape or a key or lever to reveal a secret door. We hadn't found one, but I remembered a candle in the desk drawer. I retrieved it now in the thickening gloom.

There were no matches, and I didn't have a thaumaturgy rod (a.k.a. a wand carved from the bone of a walker that allowed humans to access magic), but the transformation ritual was supposed to increase our abilities. We'd been told it would unlock power beyond the conception of most of humankind. And if a walker's bone allowed ordinary humans to use magic, surely a walker's blood flowing through my veins would do far more.

So I did as Grimwort had taught us in our Rudimentary Magic lessons. I focused on the candle's wick, visualizing it igniting into flame with as much clarity as my mind's eye could muster. And then, since I didn't have a wand to aim my magic through, I mentally *shoved* toward the candle.

Nothing happened.

I tried again.

A third time.

Then I threw the candle to the floor and slumped down beside it.

Your magic will shake the worlds, Lirielle had told me. Lirielle who was inarguably strange but had been right the last time she'd predicted something.

Yet I couldn't even light a freaking candle.

Sometime later, the two-headed golin who served as the academy custodian found me still there.

The creature was six feet tall and walked upright on two powerful legs, trailed by a long and heavy tail. Large armored scales covered most of its body except for where black fur graced the underside of its jaws and continued down its belly. Its two heads were oddly cute—with large dark eyes, small rounded ears, and long, tapered snouts that ended in delicate noses. The cuteness factor was offset by the sheer size of the creature and the razor-sharp claws on its two forelimbs.

"What are you doing sitting in the dark, dear?" asked the head on the left, Glennys. She was the nice one.

I mumbled something about having less power to light up a room than a glowworm. Then I realized the custodian's presence might mean my situation had changed and scrambled to my feet.

"Wait, am I allowed out now? Where's Ameline? Where's Bryn? Are they all right? What's going on?"

Glenn, the head on the right, curled his lip back in the golin version of a grimace. "So many words and yet not a single one of appreciation. Here. We brought you this."

They dumped a steaming bowl of stew down on the desk behind me.

"Oh, thank you. I'm starving. It's just—"

"We know, poor thing. You must be quite out of sorts. From what we understand, no one's told you anything."

"Yes. Can you—"

"No one's told us anything either."

"Oh."

"Not that we haven't deduced a great deal," Glenn added, "but we're not about to gossip with the students."

"Glenn's right, I'm afraid," Glennys agreed. "It's not our place. Besides, we might be wrong."

Glenn sniffed haughtily at that last part.

I waited until I was sure I wouldn't say anything I might regret, then unclenched my jaw.

"Can you at least tell me whether Ameline and Bryn survived their rituals?"

"Oh, of course they did," Glennys reassured me.

My heart soared—

"Only one student died this time."

—And plummeted. Like a bird flying beak-first into a window.

Only?

"Who?" I asked.

"Petra."

Petra. A scrappy girl with an affinity for water magic that I'd seen freeze the wings of a harpy-like monster to save her teammate. I hadn't known her well, and I felt a rush of sorrow for her life cut short, tinged with guilty relief that it wasn't Ameline or Bryn.

Glenn peered down his long nose at me. "One student and *one walker*."

I swallowed. Hard. But I straightened my spine and met his gaze.

The news put my own problems into perspective. They were substantial, I thought, remembering Grimwort's anger and the other professors' fear, but I wasn't dead. Not yet.

And neither were Ameline and Bryn.

So I accepted the bowl of soup and a candle, blanket, and chamber pot with what little grace I could muster and settled in to see what would happen next.

The next time the door materialized and opened, it was

Professor Cricklewood who entered my makeshift prison cell. He was carrying—of all things—a fluff ball of a creature known as a flum under one arm and a potted plant in the other.

I was huddled on the floor under the blanket, trying not to freeze. We'd just entered the last month of winter, and the weather had shown no signs of easing yet. If anything, it had grown colder. And sharing a dorm room with Bryn the firebug had accustomed me to sleeping in a room with a roaring fire. I'd also become accustomed to the luxury of my soft mattress.

"Right, kiddo," Cricklewood said, "time to learn whether we've all been making a fuss over nothing."

"Kiddo" was the nicest thing he'd ever called me. But with everything so uncertain right then, I almost wished he'd stuck to convention and called me maggot brain or something.

When I'd first seen the wizened old professor with his long white beard, watery blue eyes, and kindly human features, I'd thought he might be an ally in the unfamiliar place. He'd quickly disillusioned me of that hope, turning out instead to be a cranky drill sergeant of a teacher who hurled orders and insults in equal measure. He'd earned second place in my hypothetical worst-teacher awards, beaten only by the bored and contemptuous Grimwort.

Now he plonked the plant and the flum in front of me. The fluffy creature, which was about the size and shape of a watermelon, took three tottering steps on its tiny hooves, then sank onto the corner of my blanket.

The plant stayed motionless.

I remembered our Dangerous Magical Creatures teacher, Professor Wilverness, saying that flum weren't good for anything but keeping your feet warm, and wondered for a crazy fleeting moment if that's what Cricklewood had brought it for.

Then it occurred to me to wonder if Wilverness had meant as a living companion or skinned and made into slippers.

Damn it was cute. Dumber than a bunch of rocks, but adorable. The species wouldn't have survived in a world full of lethal predators if they hadn't evolved to taste so bad that most of those predators only tried flum meat once.

"Pay attention," Cricklewood snapped.

I'd been distracted by the fluff ball sharing my blanket but fell easily into the familiar rhythm of following orders.

"You see life force energy through your second sight, don't you? Pull it up and look at me."

Second sight was one of the more advanced magic techniques we'd been taught, and after my failed attempt at lighting the candle, I wasn't sure I'd be able to use it. But I closed my eyes and tried anyway.

"Now look toward me," Cricklewood ordered. "Can you sense where I am?"

"Yes." I could do more than that. His life force

energy shone like a beacon in the darkness. A walker-shaped beacon.

Yesterday, or however long ago it was that I'd entered that transformation chamber, my sense of others' life force had been vague, like a flicker of candlelight through closed eyelids. And unlike almost everyone else using their second sight, I'd had to shut my eyes to be able to make out anything at all.

Today I could see Cricklewood's golden energy so clearly that I knew when he leaned toward me just slightly before asking the next question.

"Good. What about the plant?"

I shifted my focus. Waited. Maybe my sight needed time to adjust to the relative brightness. Sort of like my physical eyes did.

Yes, there. A dim light, so transparent it was easily missed between the brilliant glare of Cricklewood's energy and the much weaker but still evident life force of the flum.

"Barely," I reported. "But the flum is much clearer."

Cricklewood shifted again in my second sight. And distantly, my ears picked up the corresponding rustle of fabric.

"Focus on the flum then. Can you tell me anything about it?"

"Um. It's a lot smaller and less bright than yours. But the shape follows its basic physical form like yours does."

"Uh-huh. Can you encourage it to come toward you?"

"How?"

"Whatever feels natural. Keep your focus on the life force though. I don't want you communicating with the flum or using physical magic to move it."

I tried. Nothing happened.

Cricklewood didn't give me any further instructions, so I tried again.

After a few minutes of attempting everything I could think of without eliciting so much as a twitch of response from the flum's life force, I sighed in disgust. It was like the stupid candle all over again.

The flum squealed and my eyes shot open. Cricklewood had a fine stiletto in his hand, the point of the blade touched with blood.

"What did you do?" I protested. Was he trying to motivate me?

The flum looked unperturbed now, and I couldn't see how bad the injury was past all its fluff. It raised one hoof to scratch awkwardly at its head, overbalanced on its three remaining hooves, and fell onto its fluffy backside.

It squealed as it landed, the same noise as before, then resumed scratching from this new position.

"I barely nicked it," Cricklewood growled, and after witnessing the flum's self-inflicted "injury," I was inclined to believe him. "Try again."

I closed my eyes. The flum's life force was brighter

now, as if piercing its skin made its life energy more accessible. Instinctively, I tried to gather the creature toward me, away from the professor and his sharp knife, into my arms where I could keep it safe.

This time it came.

I opened my eyes, triumphant.

Only to see the flum still on the corner of my blanket. It was lying down now. Or…

No.

Cricklewood looked from me to the crumpled body of the flum and back again. "Well I'll be damned. It's true then. You're a reaper. You can drain life force from other beings as easily as drinking from a glass. So long as they're bleeding."

I felt sick.

I'd been trying to *protect* the flum. Yet somehow instead I'd called its life force over to me and left its body behind. Killing the poor creature in an eye blink.

Which was supposed to be impossible. Not even healers could transfer life force. Their ability to heal was constrained by what the patient's life force could provide energy for.

And I had absorbed the flum's life force into my own. I felt it. My body grew warm for the first time in hours, and I was energized as if I'd actually managed to sleep. It felt good, and that made it all the more sickening.

Cricklewood nodded, a self-satisfied smile breaking across his crinkled old face.

"You're either the one we've been waiting for or a horrifying aberration that ought to be put down."

He ran a hand down his long, long beard.

"Now I just have to convince the cowards to give us the chance to learn which."

CHAPTER FOUR

I did not sleep again that night.

Cricklewood departed, thankfully taking the poor flum's body with him, and I huddled in my prison cell, wondering what they'd turned me into.

I had now taken two lives without trying to. Kyrrha's, the walker woman. I hadn't even been conscious when I'd apparently drained her life force. And the flum's. I'd just been following Cricklewood's orders, unaware of the consequences.

But I was aware now, and I felt dirty. Nauseated.

I'd killed before, but only ever as a matter of survival. There was little nature had to offer more harmless than the flum, and this was the first time I'd taken another life without good cause.

I'd certainly never killed a human being. The walkers were a long way from human, but far closer than a night crawler spider was, and like me, Kyrrha had only been following orders.

Maybe my self-reflection was pointless anyway. From what Cricklewood had said, the professors had not yet decided whether to let me live.

Which was the other reason I couldn't sleep.

I didn't understand. This was what they'd wanted. *They* had done this to me. Transformed me. Given me this terrifying new power. Terrifying, yes, but perfect for the warrior they were supposedly crafting me to be.

What the hell was their problem?

Maybe they were afraid I'd turn against them.

I wrapped my blanket tighter around me and scowled into the darkness. Maybe they were right to be afraid.

Maybe I would.

CHAPTER FIVE

Grimwort had ordered Millicent not to let me out. He'd failed to mention anything about letting others in.

So an hour before dawn, just as the section of sky I could see through the window was shifting to a gloomy gray, four figures snuck into the room.

Figures I actually *wanted* to see. Two of them at least. Ameline, my best friend since forever. And Bryn, who was fast becoming just as dear to me.

The other visitors I was less sure about. Two walker students, Theus and Lirielle.

Ameline immediately rushed to my side and joined me on the floor. Her stride was shorter, stiffer than usual, her movements cautious as if they pained her, and by the messy state of her golden halo of hair, she hadn't taken the time to brush it before coming to visit me.

My heart swelled as it always did when I saw her familiar face after an absence. Jeez, I loved her. She was gentle and generous and kind, and I wished with every-thing I had that I could offer her a world where she could be safe and happy, where she didn't have to harden her wonderful nature just to survive.

But I couldn't. And she'd proven herself able to cope with that reality. She'd charged into a battle she had no hope of winning and bloodied her hands to save our lives.

Bryn sauntered over as well, hugging herself against the chill. She was small and slight beside Ameline's curves, and her short black hair hung straight and sleek above her shoulders. But even in the meager light of the candle, I could see that her lips were cracked and her complexion was off. Not just because of the old bruise that colored her left cheek a sickly green either.

Bryn couldn't have been more different from Ameline. Bold, reckless, and often self-serving. She'd grown up rough and had adopted a take-no-prisoners attitude to her dealings with the world. But that hadn't stopped her from being willing to sacrifice herself—to be paralyzed and torn apart by beasts—to save my and Ameline's lives in the final trial.

My friends' actions in that harrowing test were forever imprinted on my heart. I didn't know what I'd done to deserve their love or loyalty. But having them here with me, seeing them safe for the moment and their beloved characters unaltered by the ritual, was a balm to my soul.

A lump formed in my throat and my eyes stung. I was so, so glad to see them.

Then Bryn set the antique writing desk on fire with a casual wave of her wandless hand. "There. That should take the chill out of the air."

"Bryn!" I protested. "You know how Millicent feels about damaging—"

"Relax. It looks like fire, it feels like fire, but it won't actually burn anything. Handy new trick I picked up recently."

"You wouldn't believe how much she's been showing it off either," Ameline added. "Or maybe you would."

We sniggered and Bryn plonked herself down beside us, utterly unaffected by our amusement. "Go ahead and laugh. I'll bask in your envy like a cat before a hearth."

That caused us to snigger some more, and Bryn grinned. She had a way of grinning that was entirely hers, the expression flashing quick and sharp across her heart-shaped face.

Ameline sobered first. "Are you okay?" she asked me. "I can't believe they stuck you in here straight after your transformation ritual without even a bed to recover in."

I shrugged. "The ritual didn't leave me exhausted the way it was supposed to."

It had energized me in fact. I still didn't completely understand why, but I'd come to the queasy conclusion it had something to do with sucking the life force out of the walker woman. Kyrrha.

On the topic of walkers, Theus and Lirielle were

hanging back by the door, unnaturally motionless as their kind tended to be.

I waved them over. "You might as well get comfortable too."

I wouldn't classify them as friends, but they'd been... collaborative rather than condescending. And though I didn't trust them, if I had to have a walker standing at my back, I would choose one of them.

"Please tell me you're here to explain what the heck's going on," I said.

It wouldn't be the first time Theus had taken the time to answer questions no one else would. But even then he only told us *some* of what we wanted to know. As if abiding by an incredibly frustrating set of rules only the walkers understood.

He'd told us the truth about the transformation ritual, for example, but he'd refused to tell us why on earth the walkers would need humans for their elite warrior unit and what those warriors would be fighting.

Theus sank gracefully to the floor six feet away and sat with his legs folded and back straight, looking like some sort of god in the flickering light of Bryn's flames. His handsome face was open and appealing, with clear-cut features, dark expressive eyebrows, and deep forest-green eyes you could lose yourself in. But it was his unusual kindness—especially rare in a walker—that drew me to him. That had formed an uneasy bond between us.

He was the walker I trusted most. Which was still

less than any human left alive on our ravaged planet. But he'd helped us, saved us, and even allowed me to see my family through a visual gateway. Some part of me I didn't want to acknowledge sensed that if he'd been a human rather than a walker... Well, it didn't matter, because what he was would never change. And right now we had more pressing concerns.

"We will do our best to make things clear," he said.

Lirielle remained standing, staring at me as if she saw something far more interesting than anyone else did.

She was slender and delicate, her features almost ethereal, with hair the color of frost and skin nearly as pale. Her smoky-blue stare was unnerving, but she was a strange sort, and I knew my discomfort wasn't her intent.

"Did you get my note?" she asked abruptly.

Her note about my wildcard magic shaking the worlds, she meant.

"Yes." I'd been encouraged by those words before the transformation ritual. Now I wasn't sure what to feel.

She nodded once, more to herself than me. "Good."

Ameline was snuggled into my side, her head leaning on my shoulder. Bryn wasn't as open in her affection, but she was still sitting close enough that her arm brushed mine when she waved her hand in a dramatic flourish toward Theus. "Please, enlighten us."

"What would you like to know?"

Good question. There was so much I didn't under-

stand, that didn't make sense. And I'd had hours of soli-
tude to drive myself mad with those unknowns.

"What's going on? Why am I in this room? Why are
the professors treating me like I'm diseased when *they're*
the ones who compelled me to do the transformation
ritual and who supposedly want us to be warriors? And
now that we've undergone the transformation, I believe
you promised you'd tell us what mysterious enemy we're
going to be fighting."

Theus took a moment to absorb all this, then said six
words that flipped my world upside down.

"You're here to fight the Malus."

What?

I shook my head, certain I must have misheard, that
he must be joking.

But there was no trace of humor on his face, nor
Lirielle's. And on my right, Ameline's expression was one
of horror.

On my other side, Bryn—Bryn who was always
fidgeting, even in sleep—had gone still.

The last, more than anything, convinced me I hadn't
misheard after all. That this was no joke.

But that was absurd. Terrifyingly, sickeningly
absurd.

When the invaders came, human civilization had
been at the pinnacle of technological sophistication,
more advanced than at any other time in history. Our
ancestors from the Before had weapons, technology, and
resources that those of us who'd come afterward couldn't

even comprehend. They'd ruled the earth, they'd outnumbered us at least a million to one, and they'd thrown everything at defending themselves from the Malus and the rest of the invaders.

And they'd been massacred.

My grandmother had recounted the video footage she'd seen before technology had failed. Nukes did nothing to the monstrous darkness that was the Malus. And any soldiers that got close—no matter what protective gear they wore or armored transports they entered in—died. Collapsing to the ground like puppets with their strings cut, and not a mark on them.

Those who lasted a little longer screamed and screamed, releasing a volley of bullets at nothing before falling alongside their comrades. Civilians didn't stand a chance. Nor did animals, plants, or even cockroaches.

The entire continent of Europe had been wiped out by that unstoppable darkness while the rest of the world watched on, helpless. Then international communications failed, and no one knew what happened after that.

The Malus was an enemy beyond my conception. And they wanted us to *fight* it?

Waves of shock and horror crashed over me until I was drowning in them. What on this forsaken planet were a bunch of barely trained teens supposed to do?

I forced myself to inhale. To breathe. Then I exhaled and did it again, trying to think. React. Reason.

The walkers who'd founded this academy must be certifiably insane.

Insane or… desperate.

That was a terrifying thought. What would it take to bring the all-powerful walkers to the point of desperation?

Either way, the outcome was the same. We were going to be slaughtered.

I sucked in a few more lungfuls of air. All right then. No point speculating when I had someone offering to answer my questions right in front of me.

"Explain," I ground out. "Human history places the Malus as your ally. Did your nasty monstrosity turn against you?"

Theus flinched as if I'd struck him. "No. We did not come to your world to destroy, but to protect."

I laughed without an ounce of humor. "Well you did a bang-up job of that."

Theus shook his head. "The Malus was never our ally. It is our greatest enemy. Our opposite in every way. We are predators, yes, but we give back more than we take. Our magic is, at its essence, that of life. It sustains life. Magnifies life. That is why nature has increased in immensity, abundance, and power. It is why Millicent is sentient. Why humans are developing their own magic. We are predators, yes, but there is balance."

His green gaze seared mine, imploring me to understand.

"The Malus. It's not like us. It drains the life force from any and every living thing and gives nothing in return."

My heart pounded in my ears even though I was sitting completely still. How could that be true? How could any of that be true?

We'd thought the Malus was a walker weapon. A terrible weapon. But the idea of it *not* being under their control was actually worse. A lot worse. The walkers, as foreign as they were, could be understood, reasoned with. The Malus as far as anyone knew wanted only to devour life with an unending alien hunger.

I shook myself, throwing off Theus's wild claims. "We saw you working with it," I pointed out. "Before our communication technology went down. Walkers seized territory beyond what the Malus had already taken over. You forced people from their homes or killed them if they refused to leave. You burned everything to the ground!"

Theus bowed his head. "We did that. It's true. But not to claim territory. It's the only tactic we know to hold back the Malus from advancing. Like a wildfire, if you take away its fuel, you can slow it down or even contain it for a while. We had to kill those that would not evacuate. If we left them, they would've fallen to the Malus and made it more powerful."

Ameline's body was trembling against mine. Bryn's magical fire had tripled in size and was threatening to burn down the wall. Or it would have been if the flames were consuming fuel.

"You're lying," I snapped. "You came as invaders. You brought thousands of creatures with you that attacked our kind. And if you do have life magic, you used it only for death."

Lirielle canted her head, her expression one of mild puzzlement. "The Malus destroyed their world. Our world. We had to bring them with us or doom them to extinction by starvation. And while casualties were high, most of the species we brought only kill in defense or the need for food. Humans are rare in that they do not follow the same pattern."

"But in bringing them here you threatened us with extinction!"

Theus cleared his throat uncomfortably. "Actually, there are still many of your kind left. And we are ensuring you and the other species native to this planet survive even now. That is where those that fail at the academy go. The Preservatorium. Perhaps—if the Malus is defeated—we can one day return the planet to a semblance of its natural state."

I opened my mouth and shut it again. I didn't even know where to start.

"I know it's a lot for you to take in," Theus said quietly, still calm and rational, like they were the good guys. Like humans had gotten it wrong for the past fifty years. "But whatever your parents or grandparents told you, whatever mistakes were made—and there were plenty on both sides from what I gather—you need to come to terms with the idea that we're now fighting the same enemy. An enemy that could cause mass extinction of this entire world."

His utter conviction robbed my fury of some of its heat. There was no way he was telling us the whole story. No way I believed this overly prettified version of history. But that last part, the part about us fighting the same enemy? The fear that if we failed, we would all be wiped out? He believed it entirely.

Which made me start to believe it too.

And even if the Malus *was* their own creation that had turned against them, the outcome now was the same. We were in more trouble than any of us had previously understood.

"Let's say, hypothetically, that I believe you." Even though I did kind of believe him, I almost choked on the words.

"If the Malus can rip out the life force from anything and anyone, if it has already destroyed your world, and you superpowerful walkers haven't found a better strategy than to freaking well slaughter and burn everything in its vicinity to slow it down, what the hell is the plan here?"

Theus gazed back, still earnest.

"It's not quite as hopeless as that. Our elite warriors have been able to hold off the Malus's advancement on key strategic fronts and even weaken it a little. And there is one way to protect against the Malus's life-force-ripping power. That was one of the purposes of the transformation ritual you underwent."

"How?"

"Your life force has been separated from your body

and anchored elsewhere, which means when you come face-to-face with the Malus, it can't just reach out and drain you. Its power is constrained by distance. Which is why the clearing method works. And why it hasn't wiped out this continent yet."

I tried to process this. "Then why not do that to every person?"

"Because we want to save *all* living things. And the procedure of separating someone from their life force is complex, risky, and comes at a steep price. Besides, in the long run, even that will not be enough to protect us from the Malus. That's why we need wildcards."

Theus had explained to us before the ritual that in most cases a student's magic would be strengthened and concentrated, greatly increasing their abilities in the one area of their affinity. But for one in fifty cases, the results were unpredictable. And for those outliers, those *wildcards*, their magic sometimes transformed into power of a type and magnitude that even walkerkind had never seen.

I grappled to understand how that applied to what we were now talking about.

"So let me get this straight. Your entire strategy is just to slow the enemy's advancement and hope that one day someone will come along with a wildcard gift that holds the key to defeating the Malus?"

Lirielle beamed, as if my anger and incredulity had flown completely over her head. "Yes!"

Theus's reaction was more subdued. "That's about the sum of it."

I swallowed. And noticed Bryn's fire had guttered out. She resolutely set it going again.

"Has anyone come close to succeeding?" I asked.

Theus shook his head mutely.

"You know the definition of madness, right?"

"Walking between worlds without packing your favorite sandwich?"

"What? No. It's doing the same thing over and over again and expecting a different result."

Theus raised an eyebrow. "Sounds like the definition of foolishness rather than madness. But I take your point."

"So explain it to me. You're saying almost forty years of stealing human firstborns and putting them through the transformation ritual hasn't gotten you anywhere close to success. What the hell sort of strategy is that?"

"First of all, we didn't steal firstborns. We traded them according to the terms of the Agreement."

I bit my tongue. Hard. Now was not the time to veer off on tangents. Even if the subject of those tangents made me see red.

"Secondly, we've been trying different approaches with the firstborns, and you're growing more powerful, more magical with each intake. We're hoping that will make the difference."

"And if it doesn't?"

His mouth tightened. "Then we die."

Something that had been niggling at the back of my mind throughout this conversation jumped to the forefront.

"How long?" I asked.

"How long what?"

"How long did it take the Malus to destroy your world?"

"A hundred years."

I did the math. It had been fifty years since they'd arrived here and overturned our civilization with unfathomable casualties.

"Fifty then," I said. "We have fifty years left to figure out how to stop this thing."

Theus shifted uncomfortably and dropped his gaze to the floor, something I'd never seen a walker do.

"Your world is smaller than ours. We're estimating ten."

CHAPTER SIX

My stomach plunged downward. All comfort I'd gleaned from being with my friends, all triumph I'd felt from making it through the trial phase of this academy, vanished.

Despite everything we'd been through, everything we'd survived to come this far, we would be helpless in the face of the oncoming disaster.

Ameline's gentle warmth would be snuffed out, leaving a void I couldn't begin to contemplate. Bryn's fiery spirit would be forever extinguished.

The news was world shattering. So much worse than anything I'd imagined. And here I'd thought I'd already imagined the worst. Thought the world had already been shattered.

We couldn't stop the Malus. It was impossible. Billions of lives had proved that.

And every life left would prove it a second time.

My heart seemed to falter.

Because when we inevitably failed, my family would die.

My family wasn't supposed to die. I'd surrendered myself to the walkers to secure their futures. To keep them safe. But there was no future. No safety.

Mila would never even reach my own scant age of seventeen. She would never experience adulthood, never realize her full potential, never learn who she was and what made her beautiful and unique. Hell, she would never even grow to her full height. And if Reuben lived long enough to marry and start a family of his own, it would be just in time to watch them die.

Grief scrabbled down my throat, scraping it raw and filling and filling me until I choked on it.

I hadn't even realized how much knowing Mila and Reuben would have happy lives, that I'd secured that much at least, had kept me going until now. Until I felt so, so deflated. Defeated. Despairing.

All my life I'd railed against the Firstborn Agreement. But this was worse. So much worse. And I didn't have a hope of stopping it.

Theus stood.

"We'll leave you three alone to process the news. I know it's a lot."

"Wait," Bryn said. "If wildcard gifts are so crucial to your big strategy, why are there rumors going around that the teachers are thinking of killing Nova? Why is she trapped in this room instead of in her bed like everyone else?"

Theus froze and looked down at me with... Was that pity in his eyes?

"You have Malus magic, Nova."

His words hit me like a collapsing building.

I had the same magic as the evil monster that would kill us all. That would kill my sister. My brother. My father. My mother.

Theus continued to address me even though it was Bryn who'd asked the question. "It's the opposite of walker magic. Of life magic. It consumes and devours without end. And every life it takes, it uses to strengthen itself. It uses the strength of our fallen against us. That power is anathema to our kind."

He swallowed as if tasting something foul.

"It's hard to describe how much we've come to loathe it. We've had a hundred and fifty years of war and death to cement that loathing."

A hundred and fifty years of war and death.

Only ten to go.

It was my turn to swallow as if tasting something foul. The movement hurt my raw throat. If Theus's story was even partially true, things were beginning to make an awful sort of sense. I recalled Cricklewood's words to me.

You're either the one we've been waiting for or a horrifying aberration that ought to be put down. Now I just have to convince the cowards to give us the chance to learn which.

My wildcard magic was of a type the walkers abhorred with a hundred and fifty years of accumulated bitterness.

But nothing else they'd tried had worked. Maybe it would take Malus magic to defeat the Malus.

Theus shoved a hand through his already tousled hair. He seemed distressed. At his vicinity to me and my hated magic? Or the prospect of my execution?

"There is one last potential issue," he said. "Although you were likely unconscious at the time, you did take a walker's life."

Bryn bared her teeth. "So what? That doesn't even begin to even the score."

Theus met her gaze squarely. "I know. And I disagree that it should come into consideration of Nova's fate. But you should be fully informed of the factors in play here."

Ameline stifled a sob and Bryn made a growling noise in her throat. I just sat there, feeling wretched.

"But despite everything, I believe consideration of the greater good will win out over any personal feelings. It usually does with walkerkind. And, Nova, it's clear to at least some of us that you're an asset. Even if you are a dangerous one."

"And if those in charge don't agree?" Bryn demanded.

Theus's perfect brow furrowed, and even the imperturbable Lirielle looked agitated, losing some of her inherent stillness.

"I-I don't know," he said finally. I hadn't seen him lost for words before. "But I don't believe it will come to that." He was silent a moment before adding, "It can't."

I was no longer sure whom he was trying to convince.

His green eyes fixed on mine, and for a moment it seemed that they were laid bare before me.

"For the little it's worth, I am deeply sorry for the harm we've caused you," he said. Then he strode out of my prison cell with Lirielle beside him.

When the door had vanished behind them, Bryn released a torrent of curses, and Ameline released her own grief in the form of sobbing.

But I was numb, hollow. As if someone had scraped out my insides and sewn me back up and I was still sitting there but most of me was missing.

In that moment, with the sky the color of charcoal, fatigue dampening my spirit, and the shocking revelations of the past half hour whirling around my brain, it seemed to me that we were all doomed to die.

And my plans to protect my loved ones, to end the Agreement, to bring the walkers down and reunite the surviving firstborns with their families, burned to ash on that impending funeral pyre.

I closed my eyes and prayed I was wrong.

CHAPTER SEVEN

They came for me an hour after dawn. Every professor at the school except for Grimwort, who was noticeably absent. Their faces were stern and unsmiling, including the only non-walker among them, Professor Wilverness, who hung back in her antlered centaur form.

Dunraven acted as spokesperson. He was tall and striking with skin the color of burnt umber, a closely trimmed goatee, and a penetrating gaze that always made me feel as transparent as a window.

"It has been decided that Kyrrha's death and the magic you possess shall not be held against you. *Provisionally.*"

My breath came out in a whoosh of relief. Theus had been right. I would not die, not today. And I supposed that a conditional pardon *was* generous, because I still held each and every student death against them.

"You will be expected to develop magical proficiency

fast and prove to us you're able to keep the power under strict control. If you fail to contain your magic, if you harm anyone else at this academy, or if you put so much as a toe out of line, there will be no second chances. Do you understand these provisions?"

My mouth was dry and tacky, like I'd eaten some of the ash from my hypothetical funeral pyre. "Yes."

"Good. You missed an assembly this morning. But after your unauthorized visitors earlier, I imagine you already know what you're here for."

I waited, expecting reprimand or punishment, but he only said, "Classes start in ten minutes."

I pushed to my feet. I felt wobbly on every level: physically, mentally, and emotionally. My purpose, the one that had shaped so much of my life and formed such a large part of my identity, was on precarious ground. The history I'd grown up hearing and my understanding of the world and our futures was at threat of being overwritten. But Bryn and Ameline had only left when the bells had chimed for that assembly, and their companionship had done me good.

The despair that had seized me had loosened its grip, and I was left shaken but resolute.

I would fight until the end.

Even if it was futile.

So I willed my limbs and my expression not to betray me and swept past the professors out of my makeshift prison cell.

Regardless of my, Bryn, and Ameline's feelings

toward the walkers, it was clear that the Malus needed to be destroyed. It was also clear that at least Cricklewood and Theus believed my unique wildcard magic might somehow make that possible.

So I would choose to believe it too. Because otherwise I would crumple in a heap and be no good to anyone.

My friends needed me. My family needed me. The world needed me—at least to try.

So what if it was impossible? My first goal had been impossible, and I'd pressed on undaunted.

I would do the same now. Even if I was only going through the motions.

Perhaps if I bluffed long enough, I'd start to believe it for real.

So while I didn't trust the walkers—didn't trust their version of history, their motives, or the limited truths they fed us—it was rational to learn what I could from them.

Which meant the game hadn't changed much. We would play nice. We would squeeze every bit of knowledge, skill, and power we could from this academy and walkerkind. Since if they were to be believed, they'd been fighting the Malus for one hundred and fifty years. Who better to learn about this new enemy from?

And then? Well, it was too soon to plan that. But I'd seen the fear in the professors' eyes. They were afraid of me. Which didn't make sense when Theus claimed they'd found a way to protect themselves against life-force-stealing magic. But I hadn't missed the bigger implication: fear meant they must be vulnerable.

So I would learn about that too. And when the time was right, I wouldn't hesitate to use that vulnerability against them. The enemy of my enemy might be a temporary ally, but it didn't pardon the millions of lives they'd taken directly and indirectly, nor all the families they'd torn apart since.

Families they'd apparently torn apart for the occasional wildcard. Like me.

Shrugging that off for now, I rushed through the hallways to the bathroom. I had ten minutes until my next class, and I was determined to spend eight of those in the shower.

As I sped through the manor, it was obvious that rumors of my Malus magic preceded me. A few human students I didn't know well gave me a wide berth or even changed direction to avoid associating with me.

The walker students' reactions were worse.

Someone hissed "abomination" as I passed. Others leveled glares my way like I was the Malus itself. And one walker, despite the inbuilt fluid grace they all shared that allowed them to run through the forest in near silence and kick serious butt in combat, brushed too close and sideswiped me with their elbow. Hard.

I didn't let it bother me. *They* were the bad guys here. I lifted my chin and glared right back.

But I was glad to make it to the sanctuary of the nearly empty bathroom. I shed my clothes and ducked beneath the blissful stream of hot water, letting it wash away my tension, aching muscles, and residual nausea—not to mention the odor after being stuck in the transformation ritual for three days and the holding cell for another. I stayed under that soothing stream for every one of those eight minutes.

Then I jogged outside to Millicent's manicured lawn and joined... no one. I halted, my breath sending puffs of condensation into the cold air, wondering if our lesson location had changed and no one had remembered to tell me. But muted voices led me around the side of the manor, and there, in front of an old outbuilding we'd never utilized before, I found Professor Cricklewood and the rest of the human students.

The class was much smaller than it used to be.

I was late. But instead of chewing me out for being tardy, Cricklewood merely nodded at me.

Huh.

Some of the kids started whispering, but I joined Ameline and Bryn and felt my mood lift anyway.

Cricklewood ignored the whispers and did his pacing thing in front of us, his voice raised in its usual drill-sergeant shout. "Now you lot know why you're really here, I expect you to work harder than ever before."

The communal groan I anticipated didn't come, and I looked askance at my friends.

Bryn filled me in. "Morning assembly was a shorter, prettier version of what Theus told us. Everyone's either scared witless or so enthralled with their new magic they think they're invincible."

Cricklewood thumped his staff against the frosty ground, only then making me realize he hadn't brought it with him, hadn't *needed* it the night he'd visited me in my holding cell. I'd quickly figured out it was a weapon as much as a walking aid, but I hadn't guessed he could get around fine without it.

The wiry old walker was scowling, his scraggly white eyebrows wriggling their disapproval.

"You might be feeling cocky after making the cut and being endowed with your fancy new powers. So let me *disabuse* you of the notion."

Five minutes ago, I wouldn't have imagined anyone's confidence would need *disabusing* after hearing about the Malus, but glancing around at the students, I saw Bryn was right. Some were barely paying attention to the lesson, too busy playing with their new powers. One kid was sending electricity crackling over his hands. Another was toying with a ball of water behind her back.

Cricklewood paused in his pacing to eyeball us. "Make no mistake, the scum that rises to the top of a pond is still scum. When you eventually face the Malus, at least one of you will wet yourselves and the rest of you will disgrace yourselves. So climb down off your conceited little high horses and come and choose a weapon."

Well, Cricklewood sure knew how to give a motivational speech.

Without any apparent action on his part, the barn-style doors of the outbuilding flung themselves open, revealing three walls' worth of weapon racks.

Our group moved forward, some kids breaking into a jog to get first pick.

"Not with your eyes, you foolish flea-feeders! Close them if you need to. Feel the pull. These weapons are special, and they'll select their wielders as much as you them. I'd prefer to go into battle backed by any one of these over the entire lot of you twig-armed twerps."

The vast array of weapons was impressive. Swords, staffs, spears, maces, flails, axes, bows, crossbows, cudgels, daggers and more in all styles and sizes. If it was good for slashing, stabbing, smashing, or shooting, it was there.

I wandered over to the long-range weapons on the left wall first. If I needed to draw blood before using my dubious reaper magic, then why not do so from a distance?

But nothing called to me.

I saw Ameline running her fingers over a slender recurved bow, and when I searched for Bryn, I saw her hefting an axe way too big for her. I winced, hoping she would pick something more suitable.

But no matter where I wandered or which weapons I inspected, my gaze kept being drawn to a long, obsidian-colored blade with an elegant but unadorned cross guard. Whatever the black metal was, it made the sword stand out as unique even among the huge assortment of weapons.

My first thought was that selecting the only black blade for myself when half the people at the academy believed I was the dark scourge of the Malus in human form was a bad idea.

My second thought was that I might select it for just that reason—to send them the unsubtle message that I didn't give a rat's backside what they believed.

But in the end, I didn't pick the obsidian blade for either of those reasons. I chose it because it *called* to me, just like Cricklewood had said. And when I did lift it from the rack, it was lighter than I'd expected. Light enough to wield one-handed but with a pommel generous enough for two when needed. The sword's length combined with my height would give me a better reach than many opponents, while its surprising lightness would allow me to wield it with speed and precision.

Its double-edged blade glinted wickedly in the weak sunlight, and I didn't feel inclined to test its sharpness.

Feeling strangely certain of my decision, I slid the sword into the provided sheath and returned to the lawn outside. My friends were already there. Ameline had chosen the same bow I'd seen her admiring. Or perhaps it had chosen her. And Bryn was holding a different battle-axe. It was double-headed and even bigger than the last.

"Right," Cricklewood shouted. "These weapons will practically wield themselves and lend you strength while they're at it. So long-range weapon holders will be learning speed and strategy, and you miserable cretins that chose close-combat weapons will focus on footwork."

———

Cricklewood was right. My blade was a dream to use, giving me far more skill than I had any right to lay claim to.

The professor had us apply a clear, goopy substance to the sharp edges of our weapons to blunt them, then paired us off to practice the footwork and combat techniques he'd assigned us. Periodically he'd shout to swap partners so we would face opponents of different strengths, speeds, and weapon types.

Bryn and I paired off first. Her smaller form and dancing feet made her a difficult target, and her giant axe smashed into my blade with bone-jarring force. Somehow my new sword absorbed the worst of the impact of each strike. But even so, my entire right arm was going numb by the time Cricklewood called for a swap.

I faced a boy with a spear next. Josef, I thought his name was. The reach of his weapon made it difficult to get close, but anytime I darted inside his guard, the long and pointed spear became unwieldy. That didn't stop him smashing the steel haft into my stomach, but I gave better than I got.

A girl with twin short swords and the ability to flip through the air made a dangerous and unpredictable opponent. And a muscle-bound hulk of a guy swung his mace with strength enough to break bones—if this had been more than training and I'd allowed a single one of his blows to land.

So I was panting but mostly unscathed when Cricklewood called for another swap and Klay stepped into my field of vision. I grinned in greeting. This should be good.

He and I had been the standout students (among the humans anyway) in nearly all the physical challenges from day one, and though he was a lone wolf, we had a friendly rivalry going on.

But Klay didn't grin back. His handsome face was set in a glower, and he didn't wait for Cricklewood's order to come at me.

I parried, surprised by the attack and the ferocity behind it. He had chosen a great sword as his weapon. Longer and broader than my own. And he had both speed and strength in his two-handed grip. Perhaps he was feeling extra competitive.

That was fine. I would meet his challenge and up it then. He wasn't the only one who'd trained with a sword before today.

The world narrowed to the clashing of our blades, mine black, his silver. The ripple of movement in his torso that forecast his intentions. The skip of our feet over the grass. We circled, and a sudden flash of sunlight off the steel of his blade made me miscalculate his next move by a hair. A slight but costly error that allowed his sword to land its strike against my side.

Klay did not pull his blow.

It smashed into my left arm so hard it sent pain lancing through the bone. Broken? Fractured?

Instead of stepping back to give me a chance to recover—something every partner I'd faced had done without needing to discuss it, this was training after all —Klay rushed to press his advantage.

I blocked the next strike. Just. And learned the bone hadn't fractured since my two-handed grip didn't cause me agony. But this game wasn't fun anymore.

Klay's expression was determined, set, maybe with a hint of satisfaction as he worked to land another blow. Worked to *hurt* me again.

What on earth was his problem? Was he angry about my new magic too? Klay had always held the walkers in higher esteem than the rest of us for some unfathomable reason, and not in the lovestruck sort of way some of the kids had either. But he was acting *worse* than the walker students. Why would he take it that far if he was only following their lead?

So the reason must be personal then. Maybe it wasn't even to do with my new magic.

I blocked another strike, and another. Losing ground

as I tried to master the pain still echoing through my arm and the greater sting of his sudden hatred.

Maybe he just didn't like the shape of my nose or something.

Yeah, that'd make for a refreshing change.

"Did I do something to upset you?" I ground out as I blocked a strike to my neck that might have seriously injured me had it landed, blunted blade or no.

But his only answer was to intensify his attack.

I fought to keep my temper in check. To avoid hurting him in return. At least not until I understood the reason behind his abrupt shift in attitude. That didn't mean I couldn't take the offensive.

My new sword sang through the air, a wicked, dark blur of motion my eyes couldn't follow. I drove Klay back a step, and another. We were down to instinct and training and the magic of our weapons. And somehow I sensed that my blade was more powerful than his.

Klay's teeth were bared as he fought to defend himself. I probably wasn't doing much to lessen his newfound dislike toward me, but right then I didn't care. I wouldn't wound him. Nothing more than his ego anyway. But I would teach him not to mess with me.

Cricklewood called for another partner change, and I reluctantly lowered my sword.

Klay did not. He swung with frightening precision at my unguarded neck. I threw myself backward and felt rather than saw the steel tip part the air an inch from my collarbone.

Freaking hell.

I growled and rolled to my feet as he advanced again. My sword was still in my hand, and I'd managed not to cut myself in my unplanned collision with the ground. Magic indeed.

I thrust it upward to deflect Klay's overhead swing and almost flung it into the sky when it met no resistance. Klay's great sword… no, Klay himself was frozen in place.

Cricklewood entered my peripheral vision and glared at us both.

"Save your bloodlust for the battlefield, *children*."

CHAPTER EIGHT

I should have guessed my day wasn't going to get any better.

Bruised and exhausted, we walked into our next class. Where I learned I'd come close to unwittingly killing everyone my first week here.

The lesson began ordinarily enough. Professor Dunraven had written three words on the board.

Know Thine Enemy.

Theus looked glad but unsurprised to see me and lifted a hand in greeting. Lirielle didn't see anyone since she was staring out the window. We all took our seats before the second chime sounded, and Dunraven rose and tapped the board with one long finger.

"This morning you learned what awaits you at the end of your training."

Probable death? I thought but didn't say.

"Every person in this room is here because of their

natural talent and magic, and by the time you face the Malus, those gifts will be honed into a power to be reckoned with. But that will do you little good if you do not know your enemy. If you are not prepared."

I caught myself leaning forward. This was what I wanted to learn.

"The ritual you have undergone prepared your bodies—so that the Malus cannot simply rip your life force from you. But I am here to prepare your minds, your souls, because that is what the enemy will attack next."

Dunraven's penetrating gaze swept over the assembled students.

"One of the greatest weapons of the Malus is fear. Fear is a disease that will kill more surely than any blade or claw. It overrides logic, wipes out hope, and cannot be outrun. Fear will follow you back to camp, it will tax you—mind, body, and soul—when you fight and when you attempt to rest. And fear can kill even those that survived the battle."

Now didn't that sound fun?

"There is no true antidote to the level of fear the Malus will throw at you. But we can condition you, prepare you for it."

That was when Dunraven pulled out a small iron chest. A familiar chest etched with tiny, delicate leaves. One that reminded me an awful lot of the one I'd broken into three months ago in the office I'd thought was Grimwort's.

Maybe the chest only *looked* similar. Craftsmen made products with similar likenesses all the time. But this chest featured the same security measures I remembered as well. The magical dragon lock turned violet eyes toward me expectantly, as if I might feed it some fresh cubes of meat, and I had a bad feeling that this was *the* chest.

That bad feeling was confirmed when Dunraven unlocked the mundane padlock and persuaded the dragon to unwind its tail from the loops holding the lid shut, because he withdrew an ebony circlet on a cushion of green satin.

Was it just me, or did it look like he was trying not to touch the thing?

"This circlet is a training tool," Dunraven announced. "A highly specialized team managed to capture a tiny piece of the Malus and contain it inside. A walker gave their life to acquire this resource. To allow students like you to build up a resistance to the Malus's fear influence in a relatively safe environment."

He placed the cushion with the circlet still on it on the nearest firstborn's table. "I say *relatively* safe because too long under the circlet's influence has driven some students mad. And if anyone were to try it before their ritual, they would risk being taken over by the Malus and used to devour every spark of life force within this academy and, in time, the continent beyond."

My palms pricked with sweat and my throat went

dry. Was it coincidence that Dunraven's eyes had landed on me during that last part?

Did he know?

I'd put that evil thing on my head. Had felt pulled to do so. And though months had passed, I remembered the horror of that smothering alien darkness like it had been yesterday. The disorientation, the forgetting of everything I was. The forgetting of everything that *ever* was—except for the fear. The overwhelming, all-encompassing, bone-melting fear.

How close had I come to destroying us all in my ignorance?

The only thing that must have saved me was that I'd stumbled backward. No. Not that. I'd *stepped* backward, and Millicent, who'd been holding a grudge against me at the time, had tripped me, sending me sprawling into a wardrobe. A wardrobe she'd considerately opened for me to fall into, then locked me inside. Boy, had I been mad about that at the time.

Except... that fall had been what had knocked the circlet from my head. Had been what had saved me and the entire academy. The entire continent.

Had Millicent understood? Done it on purpose? *Rescued* me?

I swallowed a lump in my moistureless throat, certain somehow that she had.

The first student raised the polished ebony circlet and placed it on his head. His face drained of all color, his mouth opened in an unvoiced scream, and fifteen seconds later, Dunraven pulled it off, using magic rather than his own hand.

Then he landed it on the desk of the next nearest student. This guy's scream was given voice, and it went on and on for the full fifteen seconds.

Dunraven dumped it on the next desk.

Even when the evil thing had been removed, the victims remained off-color and shaking. Dunraven might have been more encouraging with his words, but that delicate circle of Malus dampened my classmate's spirits far more effectively than Cricklewood's "pep talk."

I watched the room grow increasingly subdued, watched bold Bryn grip her desk and grit her teeth as the circlet did its nasty work, watched silent tears fall down Ameline's sheet-white face, and waited for my turn with a tight knot of dread.

It was only after I'd had it, only after that dark awareness seemed to recognize me, that a new terror unfurled in my gut.

What if it was my unprotected exposure to the circlet that had caused me to gain Malus magic?

What if I was being used by the Malus and just didn't know it yet?

CHAPTER NINE

The classroom was no place to voice my fears to my friends. So I shoved them down deep and made it through the rest of the lesson.

Professor Wilverness's class was next. And with the horror of the Malus so fresh in my mind, I thought I might understand why she, an Antellian shapeshifter—a species known for being reclusive and peaceful—was here helping the walkers build an army.

She began the lesson by morphing into a frightful tusked creature we hadn't come across yet. But one of the students raised their hand.

"Yes?" Wilverness's voice was dry and whispery, reminiscent of the wind through the leaves, no matter what form she took. And her majestic antlers changed in scale but remained constant in every shape too.

"How come we're still learning about dangerous

magical creatures when our ultimate target is the Malus?"

The creature swung its tusks around the room and somehow managed a pitying look despite its terrifying maw.

"Ah. I suppose Dunraven hasn't gotten to that part yet. The Malus has two ways of using its victims. Most often, it will rip the life force from its prey with frightening speed and use that energy to add to its power. But when the Malus needs a particular task done that it cannot do itself, for example when it is being attacked by life-force-protected combatants and wants to retaliate, it is also capable of using its prey as a sort of puppet. The exact details of how it does this are not understood. What we do know is that the Malus can take possession of a creature's life force inside its body instead of ripping it out and can then, for a limited time, control that creature as an extension of itself."

Murmurs of horror ran around the classroom.

"Mercifully, victims taken over in this way do not seem to last long. Perhaps a week at most. We're unsure whether the Malus then drains the life force as usual or if that life force rapidly degenerates from unnatural use. But in any case, you should be able to see why learning about all types of dangerous creatures is still relevant."

Everyone listened attentively—in a morbid sort of way—after that. Until the bells chimed again and we headed for Professor Grimwort's class.

Advanced Magic. The one where I would hopefully learn the control over my wildcard power that my stay of execution required.

The general mood began to edge toward excitement. Despite the bleak revelations of the day, my human classmates were excited to master their greatly increased magic.

I was feeling less enthusiastic. But since my life, and perhaps everybody else's, depended on my ability to harness my wildcard gift or curse, I was determined to apply myself with all due diligence.

I was tucking myself into my chair beside Ameline when Grimwort spotted me.

He stalked over, his manner hostile enough that I wished briefly for my new sword.

"Get out," he hissed.

"Excuse me?"

"Get the hell out of my classroom. You're not practicing the evil abomination of a thing you call magic in this class."

His breath was hot and strangely sweet on my face. His sharp, shadowed features rigid with fury and disgust.

"I will not have you endangering more innocent lives. I will not watch your repugnant magic blossom. Go outside and practice on something trying to kill you."

I stood. If there was another option available, I couldn't see it.

Ameline made to rise too, but I pushed her gently but firmly back into her seat. "Stay here and learn for the both of us," I murmured for her ears alone.

Then I walked out of the classroom.

CHAPTER TEN

I was shocked. I was angry. Worse, I was worried Grimwort was right to banish me. And I didn't know what the heck to do.

Dammit.

I slumped against the wall of the corridor, grateful at least for Millicent's silent strength.

No matter whether Cricklewood or Grimwort was right, whether my wildcard power was a gift or a curse, I needed to master it. But I'd assumed I would have help.

Now?

I'd managed to bluff my way through the day so far, but my willpower was wearing thin. Finding myself alone, the despair I thought I'd gotten a grip on began trickling back in.

Behind me, something on the wallpaper prodded or patted my shoulder. I wasn't sure which. But Millicent was right.

I'd made the decision to fight until the end. I'd stick with it.

The concept seemed so straightforward. The reality was harder. What should I do? How should I "fight" this?

Go outside and practice on something trying to kill you, Grimwort had said.

Well… maybe I would.

But if I was going to venture into the forest, I was fetching my handy new sword first.

I pushed away from the wall, offering a quiet thank-you, and went to our dorm room where we'd stashed our weapons between classes. To my relief, the goop Crickle-wood had made us apply to the sharp edges peeled off okay. I grabbed my cloak too since it was colder outside, and thus prepared, I returned to the front lawn.

The day was chilly and gray, with weak winter sun filtering through patchy cloud cover and an occasional gust of icy wind. The man-made lake that was part of the manor's gardens hadn't frozen over, so the wind rippled along its dark mirrored surface, scattering the reflected sky.

I hesitated before stepping past the twelve-foot sentinel hedge cats whose leafy-green haunches marked the edge of Millicent's grounds. Was this a mistake? Was I playing right into Grimwort's plans by putting myself in harm's way and entering the forest alone?

I suspected he'd celebrate if I died out there. And it wasn't more than two and a half months ago that

Ameline, Bryn, and I had watched another kid enter alone. The next morning, we'd found the remains of his body scattered about the lawn.

He'd been the first but not the last classmate whose life had been claimed by the forest's perils.

But I'd been in there multiple times now and survived. Not alone, it was true. But that was before I'd undergone the transformation ritual. Before I'd been given an enchanted sword or eerie magic that could suck the life force from almost any creature so long as I managed to nick it with my fancy new blade first.

Besides, how else was I going to learn?

I would be smart, proceed with caution, and stay close to the edge.

I drew my sword from the sheath at my hip and stepped past the hedge cats, a prickling awareness of danger wrapping around me. The same awareness I always felt when I passed the safety of Millicent's grounds.

My senses were on high alert as I tried to scan everywhere at once. Any step I took would risk falling prey to one of the many creatures, plant and animal alike, that hid beneath the leaf litter and ambushed unwary passersby, dragging them into the earth to devour. The canopy above sheltered strangler vines and various flying and tree-dwelling creatures that could be preparing to plunge down and strike at the soft flesh of my throat. And of course there plenty of beasts moving through the undergrowth as I would be doing. Many of them predators and all of them better evolved for our surroundings.

It wasn't like jungles I'd read about, where raucous birdsong and howling monkeys filled the air with a riot of sound. This forest was mostly quiet, leaving me to twitch at every noise. The wind moving through the leaves, a twig snapping under something's unseen weight, and the occasional death scream or savage growl of an encounter between two of the local residents.

I felt exposed without Bryn or Ameline beside me, without their second sights scanning for incoming threats. I'd only been able to use my own second sight in short bursts since I'd had to close my eyes to make out the faint flickers. But Cricklewood and the flum had appeared in vivid clarity last night so maybe that had changed.

I placed my back against a sturdy tree trunk—using our botany lessons to make sure it wasn't one of the carnivorous kinds first. With the rough bark digging into my shoulder blades, I kept my eyes open and called on my second sight.

The life force signatures appeared as a confusing sort of overlay to my natural vision. The faint light of the insentient plants was almost invisible, making them easy to ignore, but even discounting them I was astounded and a little creeped out by the sheer abundance of life in my immediate vicinity. An abundance I'd been blind to a moment ago. It made me think of Theus's claim about walkers' life magic feeding and magnifying everything around them.

Maybe it hadn't been a lie, but it didn't do anything for those they'd killed. Those they'd made vulnerable. And those who'd been hurt when they'd leveraged that vulnerability to separate firstborns from their families.

A vivid golden blur of life energy appeared in my periphery. Moving fast. Coming straight at me.

I readied my blade, the press of the scalloped bark at my back reassuring.

A giant cat shot out of the trees, enormous strides flying over the ground. Unlike the hedge cats, this one was all muscle and fur and flashing teeth. I'd known from my second sight it was large and fast, but the confirmation with my natural eyes snatched the air from my lungs.

The predator leaped. Claws extended. A terrifying snarl rippling from its throat.

My enchanted sword might've trembled a little.

But it struck true, slicing the cat's neck. Only the beast's incredibly fast reflexes saved its life. It twisted in midair, evading the worst of the blow and letting out a yowling screech that made my ears bleed—or at least feel like they were bleeding.

That change of direction saved *my* life too, the three-inch claws missing my left shoulder by a far too narrow margin.

I spun, ready to defend myself against another

attack, but the cat continued running. Hopefully to find easier, less-pointy prey.

Then somebody spoke.

Ugh! What in the fifteen flaming squares of Hellius did you go and do that for?

I spun again, searching for the speaker and finding none. I scanned for a likely presence with my second sight but came up blank there too.

"Um, excuse me?"

First you have the audacity to wake me from a perfectly pleasurable dream, and worse, you elect to do it by bathing me in blood and gore?

Blood? Bathing? I looked down at the sword in my hand in stunned disbelief and wondered whether I ought to drop it.

Don't you dare drop me in the dirt like common refuse! What kind of inconsiderate cad of a species are you?

My hand froze around the hilt. Had it just read my mind?

"The human kind?" I answered while my brain spun its cognitive wheels trying to catch up. I was so dumbfounded my statement came out like a question.

Well, I'm so glad you've got that much figured out at least. The voice was heavy with sarcasm. *Flying carrion, they don't make them like they used to, do they?*

It was fortunate that the cat hadn't returned for a second try, because even with my enhanced sword-wielding abilities, I would've been hard-pressed to defend myself right then.

"Make *what* like they used to? And um, are you… the sword?"

Yes, obviously. Brilliant deduction there. And I'm talking about wielders, of course. I was forged many millennia ago by ethereal, godlike beings that your limited functions could barely comprehend. Over eons, my makers passed beyond existence. I remained. Since then I have seen countless battles, wielders, and worlds, and you wouldn't believe how far the mighty have fallen.

"Sounds lonely," I observed.

The voice—or my sword—made a sort of coughing noise. Which I took to mean my observation struck true.

"Besides, I thought you selected me as your wielder this morning?"

At least Cricklewood had suggested as much.

Does the flame ever choose the moth? I can't help it if you're drawn to me.

Ouch.

"But you were helping me during combat practice," I pointed out.

Pfft, I can do that in my sleep. Literally, in case you didn't pick that up.

Fabulous. In that case I wished he'd stayed asleep, but to say so would be impolite. I chewed my lip. "Well, I suppose I can put you back on the weapons rack so you can return to napping if that's what you'd prefer…"

No! Ahem, I mean, never mind, that's all right. What's your name?

Ha. Got him.

"Nova. What's yours?"

Galladrius Mordenaare Kindroth Sorfildur.

I was never going to remember that. "Hmm, those godlike beings that named you had a lot of time on their hands, did they? What does it mean?"

Illustrious Slayer of All That Must Be Smote.

"Well, nice to meet you," I lied.

My sword made a sniffing sound. *I wish I could express a similar sentiment.*

I ignored this and plowed on. "I think I'm gonna go ahead and call you Gus."

Gus? Really? It sounds most uncouth.

"I could make it Mord the Sword if you'd prefer."

Do that and I'll fillet you myself.

"Gus it is then."

Gus sighed.

"Think about it as modern," I advised.

My sword sniffed again. *What's to like about modern? The godlike beings I was forged by were made of light and shadow and ether and umbra. Their enemy's blood tasted of starlight and frosted dew and the colors of creation. But the* modern *blood you just forced me to sample tastes of iron and excessively salted dirt.*

"You've only tasted the blood of one creature," I said, though I suspected his conclusion was correct.

And that was one too many.

I wondered if the godlike beings that had created

him hadn't actually faded from existence but instead left him behind on purpose.

I heard that, he informed me. *So long as I'm on your hip or in your hand, I can speak into your mind as I'm doing now and may also choose to listen to your thoughts. It's useful in battle. But fear not, both your existence and your mind's ramblings bore me.*

Oddly enough, I *did* find that last reassuring.

Wonderful. His tone was drier than desert dust. *You had best be planning on cleaning me later.*

I frowned. Of course I'd been planning on cleaning him. It. Whatever. I kept very good care of my weapons. Except for when I lost them, anyway.

I wondered if I might be inclined to lose Gus in the near future.

Then I wondered if he'd heard that.

But he *was* superb in a fight. Even if he complained about it copiously afterward.

It occurred to me that this strange and ancient sword might require a different sort of care than my mundane blades.

"What do you prefer to be cleaned with?" I asked.

Got any nectar of life?

"Uh, no…"

Essence of the cosmos?

Oh boy. "Just ran out this morning."

You're not as funny as you think you are. Milk from the blessed celestial yak?

Seriously? Was he making this stuff up?

"None of that either, sorry."

Gus let out a heavy sigh. Even though he possessed no lungs to do it with.

Then a mixture of milk and honey will be fine.

Milk and honey? I mean, I guess it tasted better than blood, but I wasn't sure what Glenn and Glennys would say when I asked them for the supplies.

I held in my own sigh. "Okay. Do you need to be oiled as well?"

Gus snorted. *I'm not some second-rate hunk of metal prone to rust if I don't get any of your fumbling assistance.*

"Good to know." I was beginning to suspect the less time I had to spend in the sword's company, the better.

And on the subject of time, I knew instinctively that I'd lingered too long. Nothing positive would come of presenting a stationary target for every predator in the woods.

It was only as I prepared to move that realization hit me. In the ferocity of the cat's attack and the surprise of my sword's "awakening," I'd completely forgotten to practice my life-force-draining magic.

Ugh.

On the upside, some other monster was sure to try to eat me soon.

Which was when I heard it. The quiet sound of leaf litter compacting under significant weight, approaching behind me...

CHAPTER ELEVEN

I drew on my second sight to get a gauge on whatever was approaching behind me. Except according to my second sight, nothing was there. Nothing close and large enough to be responsible for the sounds I'd heard.

The idea of something with the power to cloak its life force made the hair prick on the back of my neck.

"Prepare to taste some more blood," I breathed to Gus. Then lunged around the tree to face the new threat.

What I saw made me pull up short.

"Theus? What are you doing out here?"

His unruly hair and the color of his cheeks had been touched by the wind, and there was a light in his eyes that had been lacking indoors. They landed on my raised and bloodied blade, and his lips curved in a half smile.

"I came to offer you backup so you can focus on

practicing your magic. But it seems my protection might be superfluous."

It was telling that I felt relief. Telling and a little disturbing. When had I come to trust him to protect me?

"Actually, backup would be great," I said. Because I had to say something, and because it was true.

Oh please. Stop pandering to him. I'm the one that just saved your neck.

"For which I'm grateful," I hissed, "but why don't you go back to that pleasant dream you were having?"

Gus made a rude noise.

You'd think a being that had existed for millions of years would be above such things.

Theus was eyeing me in concern. "Are you all right?"

To divert his attention, I blurted the first question that came to mind. "Why can't I see you with my second sight?"

I'd learned during our snooping that the walker students were invisible to this peculiar second vision, but at the time, I'd just chalked it up as yet another mystery and not a very important one.

But my abilities had been far less powerful then, and with my wildcard magic heavily intertwined with life forces, it seemed more important for me to understand now.

Theus's dark brows rose, surprised maybe.

"You already know the answer. Like you, my life

force has been sundered from me in preparation to face the Malus."

Great. So his surprise had been at my slowness to connect the dots.

But the reality of what that meant—to have been separated from our life force—was only now sinking in.

Before it had been an abstract idea, a theoretical detail buried beneath the deluge of shocking revelations they'd piled upon us in the past week. But *seeing* Theus's body without the life force apparent in every other flesh-and-blood creature I'd looked at made it real for the first time. Made me realize just how grave our transformation rituals had been.

How was it even possible to separate a living being from their life force and for that being to go on living?

"Then how are you not dead?" I asked. "And for that matter, how am I not dead?"

Amusement flickered in his deep green eyes. "Are you so sure you're not? Humankind have thousands of tales about zombies and the other undead."

I gaped at him, and he cracked a smile.

"I'm jesting. It's complicated, but the short version is that our life force is still whole, it's simply been moved and anchored elsewhere. We're still connected to it by a thin thread of energy. If you look hard enough with your second sight, you might be able to see it."

I brought up the sight again, feeling it becoming easier with repetition, and peered intently at Theus. Sure enough, there was a delicate golden strand leading off into the distance. This was the reason we could stand before the Malus without being instantly drained.

"Wow. I see it."

I remembered the fear in the other walkers' gazes. Fear *and* loathing, yes, but why would they be afraid of me if they were invulnerable to my Malus magic?

"Can I affect it?"

Theus shrugged. "You shouldn't be able to, but we don't really know since you're the first person to ever manifest this gift."

He seemed remarkably unconcerned about the possibility.

"I might let you try later... once you've had a *lot* more practice."

I decided he must be *jesting* again and focused on the more immediate implications.

"So Cricklewood hasn't gone through the same ritual then? Because I could see him as clear as the sun."

"That's right. None of the teachers have. Hollows— that's what we call walkers who've been separated from their life force—are too valuable to waste teaching."

That explained why some of the professors seemed more afraid than the students. But it raised a new question.

"Wait. If hollows are so important, why are you all hanging around twiddling your thumbs at the academy?"

Theus glanced down at his thumbs. "Ah, I'm afraid that's a human idiom I'm not familiar with."

I hid a smile. "It means wasting time, like you've got nothing better to do than fiddle with your thumbs. It's obvious to everyone that the walkers aren't challenged by the lessons or the trials. Not so far anyway."

He arched an eyebrow. "Sometimes keeping you humans alive is hard work."

I snorted. "Tell me about it."

It was strange to share a joke with a walker. But his expression sobered quickly enough.

"We *are* at the academy for a purpose. To form relationships with the same warriors we will one day be fighting beside."

I frowned. "Then why are you and Lirielle the only ones making an effort?"

"Because most seventeen-year-olds are cocky and stupid?" Theus suggested, but then he shrugged. "They're mingling among their own kind well enough, which is part of that purpose. Perhaps they'll pay our human counterparts more attention now that everyone remaining has passed the trial phase and undergone the ritual."

He didn't sound optimistic.

As fascinating as our conversation was, I was growing increasingly uncomfortable that we were having it while stationary. I'd stayed in this location for too long, my scent and unusual behavior a call for nearby creatures to investigate. Time enough for a pack of hunting beasts to surround us or an intelligent predator to set up a trap.

It said something about how much safer I felt with Theus beside me that I'd lingered. Something I didn't want to analyze too closely.

So I suggested we walk onward, and Theus fell into step beside me. His movements were graceful and confident, and his superior senses scanned our surroundings. I did not let my own guard down altogether but enough that I could watch his face when I asked, "Can I ask you a personal question?"

Theus lifted a shoulder. "So long as I can choose not to answer."

I rolled my eyes. "There are few things walkers are better at than not answering."

This made him crack another smile, so I asked, "Why are you different?"

He didn't answer for a long time. Then he exhaled heavily.

"I don't know. I've never been well liked among my own kind. Perhaps that has given me a different perspective."

"Lirielle seems to like you well enough."

Amusement danced across his face. "Yes, but she has never been afraid to stand out or go against the status quo. I've tried to adopt her unflappable attitude but with less success."

His tone was admiring, which caused me to wonder. "Are you two together... like, in a romantic way?" I regretted asking as soon as the words had left my mouth. What business of it was mine?

"No. She's just the only one who believes I'm worth more than my meager powers suggest."

Ouch.

Theus was considered weak? Neither his muscled, athletic form nor the magic I'd seen him wield seemed to match that claim. But there was something in his statement that puzzled me more.

"The *only* one?" I asked. "Not even you?"

He hesitated before answering. "When you've been raised bringing shame to your family, it's hard not to be at least a little messed up. I suppose it's in part why I'm fascinated by human culture. Your species is much less obsessed with objective measures of success or power. Most relational bonds are oddly sentimental. And you don't perceive walkers as any more valuable than your-selves, no matter how they might outperform you at every turn. I've come to see that you have a different sort of strength. One I'd like to better understand."

I didn't know what to say. There was no comfort I could offer. Nothing meaningful anyway. A human girl telling him his kind were a bunch of bastards wasn't likely to offset his entire upbringing.

So instead I went with, "You're here, aren't you? You said yourself hollows are vital. That must mean something."

"It does mean something. Just not what you think." He shoved a hand through his hair. "Hollows are vital, it's true, but the cost of separating life force is much steeper for walkers than it is for humankind."

"What do you mean? What's the cost?"

"Being distanced from our life force strains us. It cuts our lifespan in half." He glanced at me, guessed that I wouldn't know what that meant, and added, "From two centuries down to one."

"Oh." My mind reeled, trying to grasp those numbers. To comprehend what that meant for each and every walker kid at the academy.

Let alone what that meant for the human students' life expectancy. Supposing the Malus didn't devour the entire world in ten years anyway...

"It doesn't work the same way for humans because your blood is mixed with ours, which increases your vitality and lifespan. The net effect ends up being neutral."

It was hard to celebrate the news when the case was so different for the man beside me, the person protecting my back in the forest.

"But far worse is that it tethers us to this earth forever. The ritual cannot be undone. And while we can step through gateways on this world and stay linked to our life force, if we tried to leave, the connection would instantly snap."

I was trying to understand why there was so much pain in his voice as he said this. It sounded like bad news for humans, for the planet they'd invaded, but why was it so bad for the hollows?

"I don't get it. Why is that *worse* than cutting your life in half?"

"Do you know what it means to be a walker? Or what it used to mean, before the Malus?"

"No. Not really."

"We were *made* to walk between worlds. Every part of us yearns for it. Imagine the thing you love most, the thing that gives you the greatest joy, the thing you were *born* for, and then imagine being barred from it forever."

I'd experienced something of that when they'd ripped me from my family. But I didn't say so. I still hoped to get back to them someday.

From what Theus was saying, the equivalent of that was an utter impossibility for him. And the pain in his voice made me pay attention even if I couldn't wrap my head around the cause.

"Before the Malus, our kind were world walkers. With stars in our eyes and wings on our feet, we skipped merrily between worlds, like a bird between the branches."

His eyes sparked with a fierce joy and longing as he described this. Longing, and grief.

"And now?" I asked.

His face fell, the grief winning out.

"Now we are the hollow ones. Bound to the earth but not of it. Bound to war but not victory. Bound to blood and death."

A creeping sort of horror was settling over me. The more he talked, the more it took hold. "Then why would anyone choose to undergo the ritual?"

"Few do. Most of us have the choice made for us by

our parents. Every breeding couple must offer one of their children for the fight against the Malus."

That took me aback. If they were prepared to demand that of their own kind, it put the Agreement with the humans in a startlingly different light.

"Do you have any siblings?" I asked, feeling the pang that always struck me when I thought of my own. Perhaps the night Theus had enabled me to look through the gateway to see them, he'd understood my need to know they were okay more than I'd given him credit for.

"Yes. Three," he told me. But no warmth, no joy, no love touched his features. There was only pain there.

He noticed me staring and elaborated.

"I do not enjoy the relationship you do with your brother and sister. They are each powerful, perfect, as they are supposed to be. I hold nothing against them, but it was painful to watch my parents look upon them with pride."

His usually beautiful voice, deep and resonant, was strained.

"Most of those chosen to become hollows are sent to the academy at seventeen with great honor, respect, and grief. It is difficult for a parent to select a child, knowing that their years will be halved, their life bound to this world, and their future filled with the bitterness of war. But in this age, standing against the Malus is also where the most stature can be obtained. Hollows are honored for working to restore the balance."

He swallowed like it hurt. "For my parents, the choice was easy. They were only too happy to send me off to become a hollow, to get their weak son out from under the noses of those that judged them for my short-comings. In fairness, they hoped the ritual would transform me, balance out my weakness. But when that failed…" He broke off.

Sympathy welled in me. An emotion I'd never expected to feel toward a walker. It's hard to feel sorry for someone that thinks themself superior to you. But Theus had never treated me that way. Never treated any human that way that I'd witnessed.

When he'd stayed behind in that first trial, I'd believed he'd done it for tactical reasons. To gain huge amounts of points by saving all the useless humans. But that had been my own assumption, borne out of my preconceived ideas of walkers rather than from anything he'd said or done.

Now I felt sorry for him—and ashamed of myself. Neither of which I wanted to feel. So I pushed back against those emotions, reminding myself of all the wrongs the walkers had done to us.

Except Theus was seventeen. He hadn't been there for any of it.

Dammit, I was a mess. But I couldn't afford to feel things for a walker. Not when my plan was to take them down. Not when they'd come so close to destroying our world—no matter what they claimed about protection.

Yet here was Theus, raised without love or worth,

separated from his family as I was from mine, only in a way that could never be mended. And he'd somehow overcome the prejudice and history between our species, overcome everything he'd been forced to sacrifice, and every single wall between us, to reach out to me. He was walking though the damn forest, guarding my back, with no conceivable benefit to himself.

In fact, now that most of the walkers hated me and my magic, any association with me would harm his status further.

Neither of us had chosen to be on this path. Both our lives had been shaped and shoved around by forces bigger than us. But at least I'd had seventeen good years with my family first...

And what had it cost him, really, to look at my family through that mirror that night? Had he sensed the love he'd lost out on?

"I'm sorry," I said at last, knowing there were no words that would heal his wounds.

"Don't be," he said. "None of it was your doing. And your presence in my life has brought only good."

I smiled brightly at him, but inside, my heart cracked. Because no matter how sweet and kind this one walker might be, I couldn't let him stop me from doing what I must.

And in doing so, I would become one more person in his life who rejected him and everything he'd earnestly offered.

CHAPTER TWELVE

Theus and I traipsed around the forest, waiting for something to attack.

Our conversation had petered out into a comfortable sort of silence, and now we were killing time, hoping to attract the attention of a hungry predator.

Nothing tried to eat us.

And I felt unreasonably aggrieved by the fact.

My grievance was in part because I needed to practice my magic and in part because it was a long time to lug around my naked sword for no apparent reason. But mostly it was because the things Theus had told me had put me in the mood for a fight.

I wanted to punch something. A big ugly nasty something, preferably on its big ugly nasty nose.

Anything was better than mulling over what I'd learned. The sacrifice Theus and every snotty walker student in the school had made. The revelation that the walkers were asking no more of humankind than they'd demanded of themselves. Arguably less in fact. Theus's tragic upbringing. And my inability to do anything about it.

I found myself hating the walkers both more and less. Nothing was black and white anymore. It was incredibly confusing, and damned inconvenient to my plans.

But it was impossible not to see the walkers in a new light. Impossible not to see that there were aspects of beauty, nobility, and honor in their actions. And at least equal amounts of dark and shameful ugliness, of flaws and mistakes.

Which made them seem... well... human.

Ugh.

Why did the world have to be so messed up anyway?

I supposed the Malus had an awful lot to do with it. Which brought me back to wondering about my wild-card magic. Could it really be the key to somehow turning the tide in the war? I was dubious at best.

But a sliver of possibility was better than none, and there was zero chance of my magic being useful if I didn't learn to master it.

Which was why I needed a monster to attack me so I could practice! Hence, my grievance.

When the chimes rang for lunch, I rubbed my neck, which had grown stiff with frustration. I mean, honestly, the one time I *want* something to attack and I'm left in peace.

Maybe that was the secret to surviving the forest. Emanate violent tendencies.

Theus on the other hand moved with a free-flowing grace, as if our stroll in the dangerous wilderness had soothed and replenished him. Then again, I'd yet to see a walker move with anything less than smooth precision.

"I'll join you again tomorrow," he said as we returned to Millicent's lawn. "And, Nova?"

"Yes?"

"I'm glad that they didn't... that you're okay."

I wasn't sure why he'd decided my life mattered to him, but I gave up on kneading the tension out of my neck and smiled, a more genuine one this time.

"I'm glad you're okay too," I said, hoping he'd know what I meant. "And for the record, I agree with Lirielle."

That he was worth more than whatever perceived weaknesses his kind saw in him.

His return smile cracked my heart a little bit more.

I wiped the worst of the blood off my blade and sheathed it before walking into the dining room, where I would not only find my own lunch but some milk and honey for my peculiar sword as well.

That wouldn't be embarrassing. Not at all.

At least Gus had stayed mercifully silent for the remainder of our uneventful foray in the forest. Perhaps he'd returned to his pleasant dreams.

Ameline and Bryn were already eating, but Ameline

waved wildly when she spotted me, and I saw she'd dished a plate for me too.

"Are you all right? Did Theus join you like he told us he would? How did using your magic go?"

I didn't feel like talking yet, so I brushed the questions aside as quickly as possible.

"Yes, yes, and I didn't get a chance to try. How was your Advanced Magic lesson?"

"Brilliant," Bryn enthused. Then snapped her mouth shut. Had Ameline just kicked her under the table?

"It's okay. You don't have to pretend it sucked just so I don't feel like I'm missing out."

Ameline looked at me with sympathy. "Let's just say it beats trials and leave it at that."

But something moved beneath her hair, and the hooked beak and bright beady eyes of a bird of prey angled toward me.

"Um, did you know you have a bird in your hair?" I asked.

"Ameline found out she has mind magic," Bryn blabbed. "Mostly attuned to animals, but she should be able to mindspeak to familiar people one day too. Grimwort told her she should practice constantly, so meet Pig, her practice buddy."

"What?" I didn't know which piece of news to react to first.

"I already told you I'm not calling him Pig," Ameline protested. She lifted the bird off her shoulder. Except it wasn't a bird.

"He's a pygmy griffin," she explained. "Professor Wilverness found him after a predator ate the rest of his family, and she was helping him survive to adulthood."

I hadn't known such a creature existed, but as soon as she said griffin, it began to make sense. Except Pig, or whatever his name was, looked more like a hawk crossed with a spotted house cat—or kitten rather—instead of a giant eagle and a majestic lion.

Aside from his diminutive size, his plumage hadn't quite come into its own yet, and the effect was cute and comical, not at all fierce.

While Ameline's attention was fixed on her new companion, Bryn pushed her nose up into a pig's snout and winked at me.

I snickered and felt some of the tension slip away. As much as it was disheartening to compare Ameline's Advanced Magic lesson discoveries to my own useless traipse around the forest, it was good to be among friends.

The thought made me glance over at Theus and Lirielle's table. From day one, they'd always sat alone except for each other, and I'd assumed it was by choice.

Now I saw that in a different light too.

"Would you mind if I invite Theus and Lirielle to sit with us?" I asked.

I didn't know whether they'd *want* to sit with us. It was likely better for their street cred if they didn't. But I thought Theus might at least appreciate being invited, and it seemed a small gesture in return for all he'd offered me.

Bryn raised a brow and shoved another bite of the crispy fish and greens and mango salad into her mouth. "Sure."

"That would be a nice thing to do," Ameline agreed.

Their eyes shone with curiosity, but neither pressed me for details.

"I'll fill you in later," I promised.

Then I pushed back from the table and spotted Glenn and Glennys by the door that led to the kitchen. I supposed it was a good a time as any to make my strange request. But I hesitated.

"By the way," I said in the same casual tone I'd used to ask about inviting Theus and Lirielle to join us, "do your new weapons, um, talk to you?"

I guess I was looking for reassurance that I wasn't losing my mind. Cricklewood had said the weapons would "practically wield themselves." Maybe they'd all been imbued with teaching personalities of some sort. Like the artificial intelligence grandmother had tried to explain to me once except with magic.

But Bryn frowned. "Do you mean by helping guide your muscles to wield them?"

I bit my lip. "No. Actual conversation."

"Ha, no way. It might be a magic axe, but it's still just a hunk of metal. Wait. Does yours? What does it say?"

Darn. Maybe it was because they hadn't gotten

blood on theirs yet, but I had a bad premonition that Gus was just... *special*.

"He told me he wanted to be bathed in milk and honey," I admitted.

Then I bolted from the table before my friends could ask me any follow-up questions.

CHAPTER THIRTEEN

By the time I'd wrangled supplies from the kitchen, Theus and Lirielle had almost finished their meals. I extended the invitation to join us anyway, and Theus responded with, "Thank you, perhaps next time."

The look in his eyes said more, and I thought he understood the gesture I was trying to make.

The rest of the day's classes passed without further incident. Beyond the glares leveled my way and odd whisper of "abomination" that is.

Still, it was a relief after what might've been the longest twenty-four hours of my life. The worst part of my afternoon was the messy and sticky job of bathing Gus. (If you've never tried to wash an incredibly sharp thirty-three-inch blade in milk and honey, don't judge.)

Afterward, I needed to wash *myself*. So once Bryn and Ameline managed to pick themselves off the floor where they'd been laughing at my expense, we headed to the bathroom.

Pig, who Ameline had yet to offer an alternative name for, flapped his way under Ameline's shower spray and then perched on top of the stall to preen his bedraggled feathers while his wet tail lashed back and forth. That part of him must be more bird than cat.

My friends finished before I did. They hadn't been covered in milk and honey for a start, and I'd come to love hot showers. They were the favorite part of my day at the academy, and I found them almost meditative. Not to mention handy for easing tight muscles.

Ameline called over the shower door. "We'll meet you back at the dorm. Don't stay too long or you'll turn into a prune."

"Yes," Bryn agreed. "Plus you should hurry up because you owe us loads of news and we're not letting you sleep until you give it to us."

I ignored them both.

When my skin had indeed become so waterlogged that I resembled a preserved stone fruit, I finally shut the water off and headed back to our dorm room.

After the sticky endeavor of cleaning my new weapon, I was rethinking my relationship with Gus. It hadn't occurred to me to wonder at the time of our introduction, but if he was everything he claimed—a millennia-old magical blade that would never need sharpening or oiling—why would a walker let him out of their familial armory to offer to a bunch of human teenagers?

Perhaps Gus was delusional. Perhaps he wasn't even a sword. Just a ghost attached to it.

A delusional ghost sword. Yeah, that'd be my luck.

He *was* made out of a material I didn't recognize, and I hadn't seen any rust or blunted edges or so much as a scratch on his surface. But the existence of walkers and the Malus and other worlds made it clear that there was much I hadn't seen before. It didn't mean Gus was everything he claimed to be.

Maybe I'd ask him why his last wielder or their descendants had given him up for a mere human to wield the next time he annoyed me.

No doubt that opportunity would come quickly.

I was so absorbed by the puzzle my talking sword presented that I almost tripped over a walker student.

She was lounging against the wall, slender arms folded in a deceptively casual pose, and she looked me up and down with interest.

Unsure what to expect, I returned her regard.

She was about my height and almost dainty, but body type made little difference to the strength of a walker. Her flame-red hair was piled high on her head, showing off her elegant neck and the perfect oval of her face, and though she stayed in her casual pose, there was something about her effortless posture and grace that reminded me of a ballet dancer. Captivating light hazel eyes, a petite nose, and full lips completed the package.

If I'd met her in the Before, I would've thought she was an angel. Or a succubus.

Of course, I knew better.

"You're the wildcard, right?" she asked in a silken voice that mirrored her languid beauty. "The one everyone's talking about?"

I supposed there was no point in denying it, so I lifted my chin and braced for a fight, wishing I hadn't left Gus to air-dry.

"Yes."

But the walker kept her arms folded and made no move toward me. Instead, her beautiful face twisted.

Was that sympathy? Pity?

Maybe I'd gotten milk in my eyes.

"I heard Grimwort's refusing to teach you. Tough break."

I was suspicious, but I tried to give her the benefit of the doubt. This girl was a hollow. No matter how snotty or smug or careless she might act, somewhere underneath was a kid who must be wondering *why me?*

So I didn't edge farther away or let my hand creep closer to my dagger. All I said was, "That's right."

She extended a hand to shake mine. An utterly human gesture that looked contrived on her perfect form.

"I'm Ellbereth of House Neryndrith."

Ellbereth. She was rumored to be one of the most powerful walkers here, and I recalled she'd been among those that had played games with the humans who'd fawned over them in the early days of the academy.

"Nova," I returned stiffly. "To what do I owe the honor of your attention?"

I wasn't sure whether I wanted her to pick up my sarcasm or not. So much for benefit of the doubt. But it was hard to feel anything but dubious after months of being ignored by this girl and almost every one of her kind, only to gain their notice now. So far, very little of their attention had been good.

Ellbereth's hazel eyes narrowed. "I'm here to help you."

That'd be a first.

"Help me how?"

She leaned toward me. "There's a way out, you know. To free yourself of your terrible magic." Her words were sincere. Her expression soft and inviting. "Free yourself from this academy. From ever having to dance with the Malus." She leaned closer still and all but whispered the last words. "We'll even help you get home to your family."

For a moment, just a moment, I experienced what that would feel like had it been true.

The hope.

The immense joy. Of returning to my lumpy old mattress where I'd spent so many nights curled around my little sister. Of getting to see my brother grow taller each week and being able to scruff his hair just to irk him. Of how incredible it would feel to have my father's arms wrapped around me in that all-protective bear hug one more time.

And the relief—so great I could've wept—of leaving this burden on someone else's shoulders.

It was too good to be true. I knew that. But still I heard myself ask, "How?"

Ellbereth smiled. The way a dragon might smile as a fat, juicy knight approached its lair.

"There's a procedure. Not unlike the transformation ritual really, except instead of increasing your magic, it will take it away. You'll be cleansed of the cursed dark power that never should've been awakened within you, and since you'll be no use to the academy without your magic, I'll make sure you get home. It's simple enough for me to open a gateway after all."

I wasn't really considering it.

Was I?

I couldn't leave Bryn and Ameline to face the Malus alone. Couldn't throw this magic away if there was a chance it might be the wildcard gift that could end the destruction of the Malus. And I couldn't trust this walker girl as far as I could throw her in all probability.

Which was why I asked, "How dangerous would this procedure be?"

She waved a hand. "Hard to say. It's never been performed on a human before."

That was an evasive answer if I'd ever heard one.

"How dangerous is it on walkers?"

Her smile thinned. "Risky. But you've survived

everything the academy's thrown at you so far, haven't you? I'm sure you'll be fine."

I closed my eyes. Thankful perhaps that her answer hadn't been, *no risk at all!* That it hadn't tempted me further.

My mind was made up. If there'd ever been a choice. But I thought it best not to deny her outright.

This wasn't Klay I was dealing with here. I was outmatched in every way.

"Thank you for the offer. I'll have to think about it."

So fast I barely saw her move, Ellbereth seized my arm in a grip hard enough to bruise.

"There's no time to waste. We must act tonight."

"Ouch." I jiggled my arm, attempting to loosen her hold.

But her fingers didn't relax even a fraction. And she started hauling me down the corridor.

"Let me just sleep on it," I countered, dragging my feet to buy time.

What was the rush? Did she fear if I learned how to use my magic properly, I'd become too powerful to manhandle? Or—I remembered the brief high I'd felt when I'd pulled the flum's life force into myself—that I would become addicted?

Surely one night would make no difference in either case.

But Ellbereth didn't slow down. "No. I'm going to help you now."

Even with my dragging feet, we were traveling at a good clip down the corridor.

I looked around for something or someone to turn to my advantage. Help certainly wasn't about to come from my new oh-so-feared gift that was utterly useless against hollows. But what was I going to do? Stab her with the dagger concealed in my thigh holster?

Not unless I had to.

That was when I saw the wallpaper move. Millicent.

A horned bear-like creature held up one digit on its paw. *One.* A bird with a wicked beak lifted two of its four wings. *Two.* A kraken held up three of its tentacles. *Three.*

I planted my feet just as one of the floorboards jumped up right in front of Ellbereth's boot. She stumbled, loosening her hold on me as she fought to regain her balance.

I wrenched my arm back and didn't give her a chance to retake it, sprinting in the opposite direction.

Unfortunately, I didn't get far.

My skin prickled and then a rope of magic locked around my ankles and yanked me backward. My hands and torso slammed to the ground even as my legs hauled me toward Ellbereth. Ouch.

"I was trying to be nice about it," she said. "But for all your evil magic, you are powerless against me."

And I was.

I clawed at the ancient timber floor, trying to find

purchase. Millicent lifted one of the boards, allowing me to wrap my fingers around it and cling on.

Until the board snapped in two.

Ellbereth wasn't even looking. She strolled down the corridor, certain I would follow.

I bit back a cry. Of frustration. Of helplessness. Of fear.

Dammit! The transformation ritual was supposed to make things better, make me more powerful and give me a fighting chance against the walkers. Instead, I was stuck in this academy with a terrifying magic surrounded by the few people in existence unaffected by it.

And now a bunch of those people wanted to kill me. Or strip me of the magic, which would probably have the side effect of killing me.

I wished I could go back to being ignored.

"Ladies." It was Dunraven's voice. I craned my neck to see, and the pressure on my ankles abruptly ceased.

The professor eyed us disapprovingly. I don't know what he thought *I* had to do with this, but he gave me the exact same look he gave my tormentor.

"It's late. Best you return to your dorm rooms and get some sleep."

Ellbereth smiled sweetly. "Yes, professor. Great idea."

I realized I was wasting precious escape time and leaped to my feet. "Good night," I blurted, then sprinted for my dorm room without looking back.

I expected magic to snatch my feet out from under

me again at any moment, but I made it to the familiar
section of wallpaper and offered my finger to the fanged
ruby-red serpent. It tasted my blood, and for the first
time I was glad for the layer of security. Millicent
wouldn't let Ellbereth in. Even if she disguised herself as
someone else.

I shoved through the door and collapsed on the
other side.

CHAPTER FOURTEEN

Bryn and Ameline had been about to come looking for me. But neither were reassured when I burst inside and slid panting to the floor.

Bryn's expression turned ominous. Not toward me but whatever had threatened me. Ameline's was worried.

Their moods did not improve when I recounted what had happened.

Even if they'd come looking and found me, would it have done any good? My own magic was impotent against Ellbereth, and Ameline's communication magic, for all its uses, wouldn't have fared much better. Bryn's fire was impressive. But could she have single-handedly gained the upper hand over a walker? Without burning them to a crisp? Or harming Millicent for that matter.

At least we knew Ellbereth wasn't working with the teacher's permission. Perhaps one of my friends could run to get help. If it happened again.

I had a feeling it would.

Apparently my friends believed the same. "You're not to go anywhere alone," Ameline ordered. "Not even to the bathroom in the middle of the night."

Bryn smirked. "That's right. I'd love to keep you company while you take a leak." Her expression hardened. "That simpering snot is going to come after you again. And we're going to make sure you're not an easy target."

Ameline was nodding in agreement, and I suspected dissuading them otherwise would be impossible.

I felt a pang of gratitude for that, followed by annoyance and worry. They were so concerned for my well-being they hadn't stopped to consider their own.

I both loved and hated them for it.

"We all need to carry our weapons everywhere too," Bryn continued. She looked at me. "Even if you have to give yours daily milk baths."

I groaned and pushed myself off the floor. "All right, all right. But can we take Dunraven's advice and go to bed? I'm done in."

After a brief rundown of what had happened in my own Advanced Magic "lesson," my friends assented to get some sleep. My brain had other ideas. I'd escaped Ellbereth's grasp, but I found it harder to shake off her insinuations.

They aligned far too closely with my own deepest fears.

I lay in the dark, going over and over them in my mind like a wheel spinning uselessly in the mud.

What if my wildcard magic was no gift, but a result of my unprotected exposure to the circlet? What if the Malus was using me somehow?

I had stepped through that runegate, strived to succeed in every trial, and walked willingly into the transformation chamber with three goals in mind.

One, to pay the blood price for my family to live out their lives in relative safety.

Two, to protect Ameline from whatever we'd face.

And three, to save future generations and families from the horror of having to sacrifice their firstborn child for the others' survival. To save them from the brutal marring of what should be a joyous celebration of new birth. From living under the heavy shadow of guilt and grief. And to save the firstborns from their uncertain fates.

But I hadn't known the looming threat of the Malus then.

What if my hope for a brighter future was impossible? What if the best thing I could do for the good of humankind was to let the walkers take this terrible magic from me? I knew it was brazen to dream that *I* might achieve peace, redemption, freedom. But what if my striving wrought only devastation instead?

It was one thing to risk myself. I'd been raised as a sacrifice. I'd been prepared to hand over my life to the unknown holders of the Agreement so that my family might survive, thrive even.

But now I was playing in an arena far larger than the one I'd imagined. With stakes greater than I could comprehend.

If the walkers were to be believed…

My sheets were a tangled mess from all my tossing and turning before sleep at last claimed me.

CHAPTER FIFTEEN

I woke up cold. Apparently the pygmy griffin had opened the window in the middle of the night to sit on the sill and survey the darkness. It was just as well Bryn kept our room so hot as a matter of course, or we might all have turned into human Popsicles by morning. Ameline promised to communicate our human need for warmth and security to him and find another avenue for his late-night energies.

My loyal and overprotective friends flanked me to every class and every trip to the bathroom. We lugged our weapons around with us like we were living in some kind of medieval adventure tale.

It was kind of embarrassing.

Worse, it meant Gus could make disparaging comments all day long whenever the mood struck him.

Which was often.

I felt and saw Ellbereth's gaze on me numerous times, but she didn't try anything. Not yet.

Then it was time for Advanced Magic.

I shoved my friends inside the classroom (it helped that Ellbereth was already there), assuring them that Theus would guard my back and hoping I was telling the truth.

Not only because the forest was dangerous. But because it struck me that an hour walking through it alone offered an excellent opportunity for Ellbereth or those who felt the same way she did to ambush me where help would not come.

Theus was waiting on the lawn, and I let out a breath I hadn't realized I was holding.

"Thank you for being here," I said.

He smiled, the expression lighting up his often somber features. "My pleasure."

Damn, I didn't want to return his kindness with betrayal.

Together, we passed the hedge cats and stepped into the forest.

Yesterday I'd traipsed around for an hour and only attracted a single fleeting attack. Today I'd barely pulled Gus from his sheath when a deep, rippling snarl from multiple throats made all the hair stand up on my arms.

I used my second sight to narrow in on the threat and saw a blazing light stalking our way.

Theus stepped behind me. "If you'd like my assistance, just ask."

My head snapped around in disbelief, but only for the briefest of moments—because I didn't dare lose track of the approaching energy. Damn walker pride! And yet a part of me—a foolish part—*did* want to see if I could face this alone.

I had a fancy new weapon, didn't I? And magic that meant I only had to get a single cut in before I could drain the predator's life force.

Then the creature emerged from the trees, and I took it all back.

The form was that of a shaggy black wolf. Except it was huge, easily larger than a cart horse, and mounted on its muscular shoulders were three savage heads.

Each wolf head was big enough to use me as a chew toy, and the unwanted image of being seized by all three of them and torn limb from limb flashed through my brain. Blood glinted red on their white fangs, making that fate even easier to imagine. And when I finally tore my gaze from those bloodstained fangs and the three sets of amber lupine eyes that were locked on me, I noticed the tail.

It was not a wolf's tail.

It was longer for a start, arching above the monster's back to aim forward, which meant I could see it clearly. The shaggy black fur petered out, morphing into the chitinous segments and vicious spear-like stinger of a scorpion.

I swallowed. Then attempted to bolster my courage by recalling my father's lesson that the smaller the scorpion, the worse the poison. Maybe the same rule of thumb would apply here and I'd barely feel it.

Yeah right.

Behind me, Theus murmured, "The stinger will cause immediate excruciating pain. Avoid it if you can."

Fabulous.

The creature stalked toward me, its legs bent to keep its belly low to the ground—as if it were possible I hadn't already spotted the enormous predator bearing down on me.

It was all I could do to stand my ground.

Damn. I *knew* I should've chosen a long-range weapon.

That reminded me of my dagger. It was my fifth in three months, but I was practiced at throwing it. I reached for where I kept the handy weapon strapped to my thigh.

"I wouldn't bother," Theus said. "Its pelt is too thick and wiry for a thrown blade to land."

That wasn't great news, but I only needed to draw blood. Maybe I'd get a lucky shot into one of the wolf beast's eyes. It wouldn't be the first time I'd managed a throw like that, and my odds had to be better than average since it had six of them.

The monster sensed my hesitation. Took it as an invitation. Because it switched its creeping advance into a ground-eating trot.

I abandoned my dagger and took a two-handed grip on Gus.

I suppose this would be a good time to tell you that my religion is against killing.

If the monster hadn't been speeding toward me, I might've dropped the sword in shock.

"Are you serious? You didn't think to mention this *before* I lugged you around all day and I'm about to become monster food?"

It seems more pertinent now.

I growled in my throat.

Neither the monster nor the sword were daunted by it.

"I thought you said your name meant Illustrious Slayer of All That Must Be Smote!"

Well, I *didn't choose it. Besides, beings change over millennia, you know.*

I dove around the trunk of a large tree to buy time, cussing under my breath with every expletive I'd ever heard.

Neither the monster nor the sword were daunted by *that* either.

The beast padded up to the other side of the tree and paused. A moment later, one wolf's snarling maw snapped inches from my left shoulder while a second set of white fangs snapped a hair's breadth from my right.

Hell's breath.

I was going to die unless my sword would cooperate.

But... I didn't need Gus to *kill* the creature. Merely make it bleed so that my magic could take over.

"What does your religion say about hurting?" I

asked, leaping backward to avoid another lunge by the head on the left.

That's fine.

Ugh. "You could've led with that information!"

The monster was growing impatient of my little game. Faster than I thought possible, it savaged the trunk with all three of its heads, sending splinters of green wood flying. It would tear through the entire tree in a few more seconds.

A little surer my blade wouldn't sabotage me, I used the beast's brief distraction to dart forward and slash at the nearest unprotected paw.

I sliced off a claw, but no blood dripped from the wound.

Great. I'd just trimmed the monster's toenails.

The great beast roared, apparently not appreciating the manicure. The sound was so loud it set my body quivering like a harp string and muted the rest of the world. As an added bonus, despite the remnant of tree trunk still between us, I copped an onslaught of dog breath to the face. It smelled of blood and decay and... blueberries.

The damaged trunk cracked. Then the entire tree began to lean alarmingly to the right.

I dove and rolled in the opposite direction, leaf litter swirling around me.

"What if your wielder is in a situation where it's kill or be killed?" I asked my pain-in-the-ass pointy companion.

Lucky Gus spoke directly into my head as my ears were no longer working properly.

Depends who I like more, he said.

Well *that* was reassuring. I had the distinct feeling that winning over Gus, the Pestiferous Slayer of None, would be even more challenging than convincing Millicent I was worth befriending.

I heard that, he grumbled. *You're not such a desirable companion yourself.*

The tree smashed to the earth with a tremendous crashing and cracking of limbs that even my damaged eardrums could hear, and then the monster was once more stalking toward me.

I raised my blade. "And how are you predisposed toward this three-headed wolf thing? Might I point out that if I die, it'll leave you in the woods to rot."

I wouldn't rot.

"Consider it a figure of speech."

Retreat was getting me nowhere. I had to stand and fight, relying on the magic of my weapon and my intermediate-at-best footwork to draw blood without dying first.

Or I could ask Theus to rescue me. I hadn't seen him since I'd first laid eyes on the monster, but I *assumed* he was still around.

But to ask for help now was to give up without even trying.

I angled my body at the oncoming beast, abruptly glad I'd chosen a *longer* sword. Perhaps I could keep just enough distance between me and the three heads to retain all my limbs.

I slashed as the central head lunged, lips curled back to reveal every one of its teeth. It evaded my blade with the lightning-fast reflexes of... well, a magical monster, and I wasn't sure whether to be relieved it feared my sword or concerned I'd never get close enough to land a blow.

The head on the left lunged before I'd finished my swing, and I danced back to give myself the fraction of a second I needed to reverse my strike. Neither the monster nor I drew blood. This time. But I was expending a helluva lot more energy to keep it that way. And it was driving me backward without giving me a chance to look over my shoulder.

Sooner or later I would trip over an unseen obstacle or my speed would be eroded by fatigue.

You're never going to get the chance to practice your magic if you merely defend yourself, my sword pointed out unhelpfully. *Why don't you just slash the creature and suck out its life force already?*

I darted back again as the right head dove at my unprotected side. It was like fighting three opponents at once.

"Trying!" I yelled, slashing at each of the snarling heads to buy myself another second of life. Dammit, all I had to do was nick the darn thing! But it was hard to get around all three sets of snapping jaws, and anytime I got close, I saw the freaking stinger hovering above, ready to strike.

Call me crazy, but I wasn't stoked about the idea of instantaneous agony.

Gus was right though. The jerk. I had to take the offensive, had to risk a hole in my own defense to give me a chance of wounding the beast, or I'd lose this fight anyway.

So I backed up a few more steps while I waited for an opening. Then threw myself at the monster.

My plan was to dive under the beast's three heads, between its front legs, to the relatively safe position beneath its belly. In my experience, few creatures could back up at anywhere near the same speed as they could go forward. And I would need those few precious seconds to drain its life force.

Assuming I could.

What actually happened was the creature tore off a chunk of my dominant sword arm on the way through, causing me to drop Gus as the limb flopped uselessly at my side. The pain almost made me pass out, but I remembered my dagger, and reaching awkwardly to my right pocket, I snatched it up and drove it into the beast's belly.

The wiry fur turned aside my thrust, but the point came back red.

A heavy paw smacked into me as the monster backed up. I flattened myself to the ground to present a smaller target and focused on my second sight.

It wasn't hard to see the beast's life force. It was harder not to be blinded by it this close.

I *pulled* at the glowing energy.

The monster seemed to pull back. A resistance I hadn't encountered with the flum.

I tugged harder, desperation spurring me on as one of the wolf heads snapped at my defenseless body in the physical realm.

And suddenly I was transformed. The life force slammed into my body like a felled tree. Except a *happy, wondrous* tree.

It was like the one time I'd tried coffee only magnified about a thousand times.

The beast collapsed at my feet, the amber eyes abruptly lifeless.

And I realized I was standing. My sword retrieved and raised in victory. By an arm that was completely healed.

That was when the three-headed wolf monster's mate showed up.

CHAPTER SIXTEEN

The second and very alive wolf-scorpion monster was one and a half times the size of the first.

Yet with its mate's energy coursing through my veins, I felt no fear. Every cell and nerve ending was alive and singing. My vision was clearer. My lungs felt like I was inhaling the freshest mountain air after a heavy rain. And this new beast seemed slower than the last. Perhaps due to its greater size.

I rotated my wrist, admiring Gus's wicked blade sweeping through the dappled sunlight.

"Come and get me, big guy," I invited under my breath.

The monster came to get me.

A faint breeze stirred against my teeth, and I realized I was smiling. I crouched, readying myself to spring, and waited for the rushing beast.

When it was close enough that I caught a whiff of its

breath, I leaped. Landed precisely between the creature's shoulder blades. And cleaved off all three of its heads in a single sweep of my blade.

Blood spattered my face and clothes as the headless body stumbled and fell. Everything happened so fast I didn't have time to consider taking its life force too.

Then Theus was there, his eyes wide. "Stars and suns, that was… something. How do you feel?"

I took stock, puzzled by his reaction. Until my thoughts caught up with my body's actions.

I had just leaped eight feet high to land with perfect precision upon a charging predator's back and then lopped off three heads in one stroke. No matter how slow the monster had been, that was impossible.

And now as I watched Theus, who also appeared to be moving more slowly than usual, I wondered if it wasn't everyone else who'd slowed down but me who'd sped up.

I was panting but unharmed despite the savage wound I'd taken a few minutes prior. And energy still buzzed beneath my skin like a million wasps that wouldn't be ignored. Except good wasps.

I didn't know how I felt about that. Didn't know how to answer Theus's question.

Slowly I wiped the blood from my face, wondering if I'd need to bathe my skin in milk and honey too.

Which was when I remembered.

"Um, sorry, Gus. I know you said your religion was against killing…"

Did swords even have religions? Who founded them? Propagated them? Could Gus speak to other weapons?

Yes, well, he said, sounding reluctantly impressed. *That was a feat worthy of an exception.*

CHAPTER SEVENTEEN

The bells chimed before I'd had a chance to collect myself. And when Theus and I returned to the academy grounds, we found everyone assembled on the lawn at the edge of the perfectly round lake.

I glanced down at my uniform, which was soaked liberally in blood, and felt my stomach turn over. Looks like I wouldn't get a chance to change.

Resigned, I joined Bryn and Ameline, whose eyes widened at my state (even the pygmy griffin appraised me with uncommon interest). But there was no time for conversation.

All the teachers were out here with us, and the only times that had happened before were for the life-and-death trials that had required a lot of magic to set up. I'd thought we were done with those.

Apparently not.

Dunraven raised his voice, and everyone fell silent to listen.

"On your first day at the academy, we told you that walkers and humans would be expected to work together." He let his gaze pass over each of us and then grimaced. "So far, this has been met with only the most feeble of efforts. From this day forward, that has to change."

My eyes flicked to Theus and Lirielle. I didn't mind working with them. But I couldn't imagine anything "changing" with the likes of Ellbereth.

"Make no mistake," Dunraven continued, "on the battlefield, you will live or die by the cohesion of your unit. And this world will live or die by your unit's efficacy. So you *must* leave your differences, your grievances, and your history behind and learn to trust one another. Because your life and that of others will depend on the faces you see around you today."

I realized then why in all our trials we had never fought one another. Competed, yes, but never fought.

"That interdependency and trust starts now."

At this pronouncement, the surface of the lake trembled and then the water level started dropping. Rapidly.

It was soon apparent that the sides of the lake were no more natural than its too-perfect shape. Smooth ivory-colored stone walls revealed themselves as the water drained away. Lower and lower until the smooth surface altered into stylized carvings of battle scenes. Some sort of trailing waterweed with small star-shaped leaves clung to the rock here and there, but aside from that, the ivory walls were strangely clean.

Dunraven waited for the gasps and whispers to subside before speaking again. "Inside the arena, any wound sustained by your teammates will be made real in your own flesh. So work together. Communicate. And protect each other as if your life depends on it."

Here, Cricklewood, who was leaning on his staff beside Dunraven, cracked a toothy smile. "Because it does."

The old professor pointed at three nearby kids. Two walkers, one human. "Let me demonstrate."

The three unlucky students stepped forward, and Cricklewood snapped some sort of bracelet around each of their wrists. The bands resized themselves to fit. Or to prevent their wearers from taking them off.

While the last kid was still staring at their new piece of jewelry, Cricklewood withdrew a stiletto (one I recognized from that night with the flum) from his sleeve and sliced the boy's cheek.

It was only a small cut. Half an inch long and just deep enough to bleed. But that damn gash was mirrored exactly on the other two students' cheeks.

Murmurs rippled through the crowd. Even the hollows reacted this time, while the sudden draining of the lake had elicited no response from them.

Cricklewood thumped his staff on the ground. "What are you all just standing there for? Everyone get your bigoted, grudge-grasping goat brains up here so we can divide you into trios."

Well, it was nice Cricklewood spoke the same way to the walker kids as he did the humans.

I stepped forward with everyone else but somehow wound up at the front. Cricklewood gave me an odd look and snapped a copper-colored band on my wrist. "Your group can go first."

He nudged me toward the gaping pit where the lake had been. Or the arena as Dunraven had called it. I wasn't sure how I was supposed to get down until I drew close enough to clear the rim and saw the narrow staircase hugging the rounded wall.

All right then.

I trotted down the steps, drawing Gus as I went. Two walkers, both tall, bright, and handsome and wearing identical bands to my own followed.

When my boots touched the sandy floor—sand that was perfectly dry, I noted—I stopped and looked around. The circular space was about sixty yards in diameter with the ivory walls stretching four or five times my height above me. On a section of the wall that had been hidden from my prior vantage point, there was a rack of giant weapons too large for a human or walker to wield. Huh.

A thud sounded from above and echoed around the cavernous space. I craned my neck upward to see Cricklewood peering down at us.

"Ready?"

There was no opportunity to ask *for what?* Because a noise like the grinding of giant rocks set my teeth on edge, and then the earth began to shake.

But the walls of our little sinkhole were not collapsing.

Instead, a dozen hulking creatures of mud and stone and various organic materials erupted from the sandy floor. They were vaguely humanoid in shape, with shadowed depressions for eye sockets and lumpy protrusions for noses. One was made up of mostly tree roots with a sharp beak of a mouth and long arms that ended in oversized clawlike hands. Another was all stone with a craggy brutish face and giant boulders for fists. A third had a moss-covered skull for a head, two vicious horns, and an extra set of arms.

A quick check with my second sight confirmed my suspicion. They were not alive. Held together and animated by magic alone. But the weapons they collected from the walls looked real enough. And I was willing to bet their ability to harm was plenty real too.

If I hadn't just decapitated a three-headed wolf monster, I would've been worried.

"Good news, Gus," I murmured conversationally. "These guys aren't alive, and they don't even have any blood you'll need to taste."

I'd jump for joy, but unfortunately I don't have any legs, he informed me, his humor as dry as his blade was sharp.

In perfect sync, the golem creatures turned their

misshapen heads toward us, their eye sockets fixing with unerring accuracy on me and my teammates.

The two walkers stepped in front of me. Tall, bright, and handsome number one pushed me backward while number two faced the golems.

"What the heck did you do that for?" I growled.

Number one pushed me again so that my back hit the ivory wall. "You can thank us later."

I would have liked to shove his head up his ass, but the band on my wrist put a real dampener on that idea.

Tall, bright, and handsome number two turned to glower. "Just stay back where it's safe and try not to get in our way or get yourself killed."

Arrogant jerks. Screw that for a plan.

The magical constructs charged. The sound of shifting earth and grinding stone and creaking wood accompanied their movement. Despite their size and ponderous appearance, they did not lack for speed.

I didn't hesitate. I kicked off the wall, executed a perfect somersault over my condescending comrades' heads, and ran to meet the oncoming assault with a feral grin.

My sword caught the leading golem's giant mace, diverting the stroke that might've smashed my skull like an overripe watermelon, and in one fluid motion, I raced up his body like a monkey up a tree. His knee provided a launch pad, his craggy side plenty of handholds, his elbow a useful swing, and in no time at all I was standing on his immense shoulders.

Then I swung my sword at his rocky neck.

I expected resistance. Gus was a blade I'd never seen an equal to, but stone was stone after all.

The golem's neck gave way like butter.

A glance at my "comrades" showed they had yet to move from their starting positions.

I leaped from my first conquest's falling form to the next golem before I could lose too much height and repeated my new favorite sword stroke.

It felt amazing. Like a choreographed dance my body knew all the moves for without my brain even having to engage. And the movement, the performance, soothed the buzzing wasps under my skin. They loved it, reveled in it. So I did too.

It took mere seconds before every golem lay in formless piles upon the arena floor.

My companions were gaping at me.

I was spattered in mud and clay and their blades weren't even dirtied.

They were probably offended that I'd *aided* them without their permission. Walkers hated accepting help or being rescued. Theus had explained it to me as a culture thing where honor was everything and weakness was despised.

Served these two right.

I smirked at them both and left them to lick their wounded egos as I made my way out of the arena.

But my smug satisfaction drained as rapidly as the water when I crested the rim and saw the rest of the academy. Hollows. Humans. Teachers. Many of whom were scared of my new power and wanted me dead rather than to remain in possession of it.

They now stared at me in stunned silence. Like I might be more monstrous than the animated beings I had felled.

And then the whispers started.

My eyes were involuntarily drawn to Ellbereth's.

Her gaze was full of promise.

Without taking her eyes off me, she murmured something to her companions. As one, six heads nodded.

Crap.

Lirielle chose that moment to stand—oblivious as usual to the reactions of everyone else and the thick tension that had stolen over the assembly.

"That," she declared loudly, "was awesome."

CHAPTER EIGHTEEN

There was a cost to my new magic. A steep one.

A lesson I learned with a vengeance a few hours later.

And that was not even counting the inevitable reckoning when Ellbereth and her followers made their next move.

For every ability and sense I'd had enhanced by the influx of life force, the withdrawal was tenfold worse. I'm pretty sure I wasn't actually blind, but it hurt so much to open my eyes I might as well have been. And I couldn't keep anything in my stomach, not even water.

Over those long, crawling minutes, I would have done almost anything to make the pain go away. But I drew the line at killing Ameline's pygmy griffin, and I was in no shape to drag myself out to the forest to find other prey.

I gained a sudden empathy for anyone who'd ever

battled with an addiction. Grandmother had told me there were all types of addiction in the Before, and I'd seen firsthand they hadn't gone away. Only the substances had changed.

But mine was the first I'd heard of that required sucking the life force from someone.

Well, unless you counted vampires anyway, and as far as I knew, they were still fictitious.

I groaned. Then stopped because even that hurt.

That was the first hour.

The second hour was better. Like being thrown into a pit of fire ants is better than being eaten from the inside out by subcutaneous beetles.

I wondered if the Malus experienced the same withdrawal symptoms. If that was the reason behind its insatiable appetite for life energy. Could all that destruction —the devouring of entire worlds if the walkers were to be believed—really be caused by something so basic?

If the withdrawal became worse the more life force you took or the longer you avoided enduring it, could the Malus die of shock if we starved it?

Could I?

But no, the walkers had already tried that.

Sometime around the sixth hour, my brain was functioning well enough that I came to a few realizations.

That night after Cricklewood's visit in my makeshift prison cell, I'd thought I'd felt sick over what I'd done to the flum, but at least some of my nausea must have been because its modest energy had quickly worn off and my body had gone into withdrawal. It had been far, far more mild than this. So the severity of the withdrawal must depend on the amount of life force I'd pulled into myself.

Except what about Kyrrha, the walker woman who'd performed my ritual? The woman my professors blamed me for killing. She was vastly more powerful than the flum, which meant the blood exchange must have made it work differently, her blood in my veins offsetting the withdrawal somehow.

Or—for all I knew—I'd never taken her energy.

Or I had, but it had mostly worn off before I woke. Bryn told me my ritual had lasted the longest of all the students, and I'd been locked in that chamber for three days. Maybe that was why I'd woken feeling good but without the potency of the wolf monster's energy.

I shrugged away the uncomfortable subject of Kyrrha's death. I was feeling plenty uncomfortable enough as it was. And if there was one thing anyone who lived in our post-invasion world knew, it was that you couldn't change the past.

So there was no point dwelling on it.

Of course, my future wasn't looking a whole lot better right now. Just what was the point of my new magic anyway?

With the high long gone, so too was my excitement.

It was all very well to gain amazing fighting abilities, but that wasn't what our world needed. The walkers were already incredible warriors. If that had been all that was required to defeat the Malus, the war wouldn't have spanned a hundred and fifty years.

We needed to be competent enough to defend ourselves, yes. But that was it. Physical prowess alone would never overcome the Devourer.

So what would? Was I supposed to cut the Malus, make it bleed, and then try to suck all that life force it had gathered over a hundred and fifty years?

Did it even have blood?

I remembered the resistance of the three-headed wolf monster's energy and didn't think it would be that simple. If it came to a magical wrestle over life force, the Malus would win.

And if for some reason *I* won, I suspected the withdrawal from that much power would kill me.

I groaned and turned over in my sweat-sodden sheets.

Whether I wanted to or not, I would find out eventually.

So long as my provisional pardon wasn't revoked and Ellbereth and her cronies didn't kill me first.

CHAPTER NINETEEN

I was weak but upright by morning. I managed to eat some fresh berries and drink fennel ginger tea. Even more worth celebrating, I managed not to throw them up afterward.

I felt much less excited about weapons practice.

Poor faithful Ameline wasn't looking a whole lot better than me. She'd stayed up most of the night, listening to me moan, pressing cool washcloths against my forehead and changing out buckets I'd vomited into.

Gus on the other hand, bathed in his favorite milk-and-honey concoction and with no ill effects from yesterday's feats, was far too chipper.

I've had wielders who fought unceasing battle for seven days and seven nights and they pulled up with less drama than you did.

I wasn't sure I could deal with his attitude this early in the morning.

"Yeah well, I've had blades that I kept far longer than seven days and seven nights without wanting to throw them in the river. What's your point? Besides, how did that work if you didn't let them kill anyone?"

That was before I'd embraced my religion.

I rolled my eyes so hard it hurt. Or maybe everything just hurt.

We were walking to weapons practice, Bryn and Ameline once again flanking me. And I couldn't help but compare Ameline's bundle of fluffy and feathery cuteness to my own self-important companion.

"What do you talk about with Pig?" I asked.

He was sitting on her shoulder, cat claws digging into her uniform for grip and his scraggly wings lifting occasionally for either balance or imagined flight.

"I'm *not* calling him Pig," Ameline reiterated for what must have been the dozenth time.

In truth, after seeing him guzzle down smoked fish at breakfast, I thought the name kind of suited him. But my loyalty lay with Ameline.

"Ah, sorry. Do you have any ideas for what you might name him?"

"Um…"

"How about Featherhead?" Bryn suggested. "Or Meow?"

Ameline huffed and scratched the tiny griffin's neck. "Just ignore her. You deserve a dignified name."

The hawkish eyes slitted with pleasure while the catlike tail swished.

After dubbing my sword "Gus," I wasn't sure I was any better at names than Bryn was, but Ameline seemed stuck on ideas, so I asked, "What about Griff? That's a real name at least."

Ameline chewed her lip. "I don't know. Griff the pygmy griffin?"

"Better than Pig the pygmy griffin," I pointed out.

Bryn shot us a mock glare. "Hey, that's a matter of opinion, and I'll thank you not to insult my personal preferences."

Ameline sighed. "All right. Let's go with Griff before Pig gets any more entrenched."

The griffin ruffled his feathers in apparent agreement.

Bryn shrugged and trailed her fingers lovingly over her battle-axe. "At least I got to name my own weapon."

"Oh?" I asked. "What have you called it?"

"Choppy."

We were all smiling when we reached the lawn and spotted Cricklewood.

But mine faded as Klay's angry gaze locked on me. My unwise display of my power yesterday had likely poured gasoline on his newfound hatred. And he was doubtless feeling fresh and perky. Could I protect myself from him when my legs were still wobbly?

A bunch of the other kids were stealing glances at me too. And I realized that even for those who thought my magic was enviable rather than evil, I'd painted myself as the student to beat. For the boasting rights of defeating the golem slayer if nothing else. Which meant they would all be extra eager to grapple with me and win. Just when I felt least capable of dealing with it.

I resolved to fight Klay first, before what little strength and stamina I had gave out.

Cricklewood had us reapply the edge-blunting goop to our weapons, and I kept an eye on Klay to make sure he did his properly. I was pretty sure he only wanted to hurt rather than kill me. After all, he hadn't used his magic to gain the upper hand or tried for a thrust that would've been lethal even with the goop. But I wasn't going to chance it.

When Cricklewood ordered us to pair up, I made straight for Klay and hoped I wasn't making a grave mistake. There was a gleam of anticipation in his angry stare.

My plan was to go in hard and fast and win the fight before it really had a chance to start. I just didn't know how I was going to pull that off.

I know a good trick to help, Gus volunteered.

I weighed my sword's offer as Klay lifted his own sword in readiness. Should I be suspicious or grateful? I *had* cleaned him before my withdrawal began, so that was a point in my favor. On the other hand, he'd been no more impressed with the taste of mud and stone golems as he'd been with the taste of wolf-scorpion-monster blood, so he might be cranky. And I *had* sort of threatened to toss him in a river a few minutes ago…

Gus sniffed. *You're making me cranky by doubting my noble intentions.*

Since I had no way of knowing when Gus was monitoring my thoughts or preoccupied with his own, I felt the need to respond aloud.

"All right. Let's do this."

With luck, Klay would think I was talking to him and Gus would understand otherwise.

Follow my lead.

Gus grew abruptly heavier, a *lot* heavier, and with the balance completely off.

What the?

Cricklewood ordered us to fight, and Klay came at me. Under the guidance of my brilliant, millennia-old, gods-forged sword, I stumbled forward, lost control of my blade, and plunged it point-first into the grass.

"Good trick," I muttered dryly. "You can stop helping at any time."

But as I wrenched the blade free of the soil to meet Klay's strike, a clod of dirt hit him square in the face.

It was a dirty tactic but an effective one. I rushed to take advantage, dodging Klay's now-blind swing, tripping him on his own forward momentum with the flat of my blade, and following his descent to the earth to press Gus's point against his throat.

Well, we'd never been told to stick to "proper" swordsmanship. There was no such thing in battle.

"What the hell is your problem?" I growled, shoving Klay's shoulder with my boot so I could see his face for this exchange. Because I was damn well going to make sure we *had* an exchange now that he was at my mercy.

Klay stayed silent but gave me a glare worth a thousand words. He'd always been hard to pull into conversation, but this was ridiculous.

"I'm not letting you up until you explain yourself," I said, readjusting the tip of my blade against his throat. Sure, it was dulled with goop, but it was still dangerous with enough pressure.

"I know words are hard for boys who haven't grown into men yet, but go ahead and try."

More hostile silence.

I was getting seriously fed up now. "What have I ever done to you? I thought we had a friendly competition going on."

"That was before you had Malus magic!" Klay spat, more venom in that one sentence than I'd heard from him in the three grueling months at the academy.

"Magic I'm going to use *against* the Malus," I pointed out.

"Ignorant idiot, you know nothing!" His face was twisted with hate. "You have no idea about the evil of the magic you wield. No idea what you're up against."

"And you do?"

"I've seen it," he said as if this too was somehow my fault. "Seen it kill my parents right in front of me."

Crap. But I was too angry at him not to ask, "Then how come it didn't kill you?"

"Because"—he was forcing each word through

gritted teeth—"a hollow frontline unit snatched me up before it reached me."

Oh. Well that explained a lot. Why he'd been more familiar with the academy than the rest of us. Why he respected instead of despised the walkers. Why he never once complained or seemed angry about what they were putting us through.

I withdrew Gus and let Klay up. "I'm really sorry about your parents. But the walkers have been fighting the Malus for a hundred and fifty years. If they think they might need a gift like mine to turn the tide, who are you to decide otherwise?"

His only reply was a grunt. But he didn't lunge at me when I released him, and I thought maybe, just maybe, his scowl softened a smidge.

CHAPTER TWENTY

After weapons training, it was a relief to sit in a classroom and have to wield nothing more than my pen.

Even if I could feel Ellbereth's eyes boring into my
back.

Unfortunately, my reprieve lasted only until it was
time for Grimwort's Advanced Magic class.

The last thing I felt like doing was traipsing out to
the forest and using my new magic. But to my guilty
dismay, Theus *and* Lirielle were waiting on the lawn for
me to do just that.

Theus gestured at the ethereal walker girl. "I invited
Lirielle to join us today. I thought it might be wise after
everyone's reaction to your performance in the arena."

Lirielle beamed at me. "Oh yes, that was brilliant."

Either she didn't grasp that I was now in more
danger than at any other time since arriving at the

academy or that fact had no bearing on her appreciation.

"Thank you," I said to both of them, meaning the words. Except their presence meant I couldn't crawl back to bed and just pretend I'd practiced my magic.

My brain scrambled for an alternative plan. One that wouldn't risk another night in withdrawal. Should I stick to smaller prey? Those with weaker life forces? Or... I remembered the plant Cricklewood had carried into my makeshift prison cell. Had he thought I might be able to draw from that too? The Malus was undiscriminating in *its* victims.

"I thought I might experiment with botanical life force today."

It wasn't a complete cop-out. Now that I had a basic understanding of how my gift worked, it was sensible to learn whether I could draw from other sources.

Theus nodded in easy acceptance. "All right. But we should still go into the forest. Neither Millicent nor Glenn and Glennys will be happy if you put dead patches in the lawn or destroy their flower beds."

Hard to argue with that.

So a few minutes later I was outside the academy grounds, staring at a small sapling like it might make a sudden move. I'd managed to isolate its faint light in my second sight, and that done, I cut into its slender trunk stem until sticky sap oozed to the surface. Sap was the lifeblood of a tree after all, right?

Well, this is a dangerous foe if I've ever seen one, Gus commented.

Perhaps I should've used my dagger, but I'd wanted to be ready in case we were attacked in the middle of my experiment.

"Shut up, I'm trying to concentrate."

Luckily by now, Theus had grown used to me muttering to my sword, and chances were Lirielle wouldn't think it strange in the first place.

I can see why you have so few friends.

"Still more friends than you."

I'm rather constrained by the fact I can only speak with my wielder. What's your excuse?

I growled. Gus snickered.

But the faint light of the sapling had not grown brighter since the cut.

I tried to draw on the energy anyway.

Tried and failed.

It wasn't like the resistance I'd felt with the wolf monster. I just didn't feel anything at all. Like I could not so much as touch the sapling's life force. Let alone grasp it and merge it with my own.

"I don't think this is going to work," I said in a louder voice so Theus and Lirielle would know I was talking to them. "But maybe I'll try a carnivorous plant, just in case."

I searched for a tree that glowed brighter than the rest. There were several varieties that were more sentient, more magical than others, and they were known for the way they hunted, dragging their hapless victims into the earth still breathing to nourish their roots. One of those would do nicely.

The trick would be conducting the experiment without the tree getting me first. I wished again for long-range weapon—or maybe a piece of string to attach to my dagger so I might drag it back after throwing it.

With a sigh, I tried to discern which amid the jumble of hazy, glowing roots beneath the soil belonged to my chosen target and edged closer, sword at the ready. Even with my second sight, trying to preempt the tree was going to be near impossible. There were too many roots to keep track of, and when the tree struck, it would do so swiftly. Attempting to monitor them all at once was making me dizzy.

Had that one just moved? Or—

"Somebody's coming," Lirielle announced, just as a root erupted from the earth and snaked around my ankle. I sliced it in half before it could drag me far, but the tree's magic had already shifted the soil to bury my foot. I wrenched back, trying to free myself as another root came at me. I cut that one too, sending it recoiling, and tried to grasp the tree's life force with my magic.

Nothing.

I slashed another two roots and yanked my foot harder. The earth released me and I fell backward, landing in an undignified heap on my butt.

Gus snickered.

I ignored him, brushed myself off, and moved to

join Theus and Lirielle, who were staring into the forest toward whomever they'd determined was a greater threat.

Ellbereth? Her cronies? Some new enemy I'd made from my display in the arena? Klay?

We waited.

Then Fletcher emerged from the trees and I forgot to breathe.

Lirielle raised her sword.

"No, it's okay," I said quickly. "I know him. Could you um, give us some space, please?"

Theus gave me a sharp look but acquiesced. And then I walked on trembling, wooden legs to greet my childhood friend.

The boy next door, the one I'd laughed with, played with, gotten into trouble with. The golden-hearted gentle giant who'd always been there when I needed him. Until he'd stepped through that runegate to honor the Firstborn Agreement two years before I had and left a gaping hole in my life. One I'd hoped might be filled when I stepped through the runegate myself.

But that distant hope hadn't eventuated. There'd been no sign of him or any other prior intake of firstborns. And then when Millicent had snuck me through her hallways in the middle of the night to catch a glimpse of him at last, he'd been a heartbreaking meld of the boy I'd remembered and an utter stranger.

"Nova." My name across his lips was half statement, half question.

"Fletch?" My own voice was sort of squeaky. There was so much I wanted to say, to ask, to do, but I was all too aware of the distance between us. A few mere feet, and two years of the horrors he'd lived through on the war front.

My eyes raked over him, noting again the new muscles, the extra inch of height, the small scar above his right eye, the black hair that was longer than he used to keep it. But it was the lack of warmth in those dark brown eyes that made my heart ache.

He did not move to embrace me, so I refrained too, standing so close to the person I'd missed so much, with my arms hanging stiff and awkward at my sides.

"How... Are you all right?" I finally asked.

"I am alive," he stated flatly. There was no sign of his good nature or the affection I associated with him.

But unlike the bleak dullness I'd spied in Millicent's hallway, there was life in those eyes now. A wild, strange, perhaps desperate sort of life.

"Is it true?" he asked. "That you have magic capable of manipulating life force?"

I swallowed, uncertain of what he wanted to hear. Uncertain about the man—because he was a man now, not a boy—before me. Of what he would do if I gave him the wrong answer.

The only thing I knew for sure was that my wildcard gift had a way of polarizing people. Hate or hope. And I didn't know which side Fletcher would fall on.

I must have stayed silent a long time, because he

reached out then, his large hands wrapping around my stiff, awkward arms, and shook me. Gently, but with an impatience that was new.

"Tell me."

My hand touched Gus's hilt for reassurance. A tiny gesture that felt like a betrayal of everything we'd once shared. "It's true," I admitted, bracing myself for his reaction.

His eyes—his beloved brown eyes that were both so familiar and so foreign at the same time—lit.

Hope then.

"I always knew you were special," he breathed, and for a moment I thought I glimpsed my old friend lurking deep inside the stranger. "When you graduate, I want you to join my unit. The Raptor unit. Promise me you'll request it."

My head spun, but I nodded. "I pr-promise."

He squeezed my arms where he'd gripped them to shake me seconds earlier. "I must go. But, Nova, I'm so glad you're here. That you made it through. Seeing you again is like glimpsing the sun after months of darkness."

I swallowed, unshed tears stinging my eyes, and watched him until he disappeared.

That was the best part of my day.

CHAPTER TWENTY-ONE

Ten days passed before Ellbereth struck.

I was fast asleep when it started. The first I knew of anything amiss was when something scuttled across my face.

Only semiconscious, I brushed it off. Then sat bolt upright, searching in the glow from the fireplace for whatever had woken me. If that had been a bug, it had been *huge*.

I spotted it when the thing darted over my sheets and jumped for my face again. A white spider the size of my palm.

I managed not to shriek. Barely. And swatted it away mid-leap.

This time I saw where it fell. And as I watched the eight-legged arachnid struggle to right itself, I realized two things.

One, it was faintly luminescent.

Two, it was made of paper.

When it came at me a third time, I caught it.

The spider unfolded itself in my hands. The crinkled but flat square of paper I was left with contained a note. And now I understood the reason for its luminescence. Ellbereth had considerately included that magical feature so I could read her demands without turning on a light.

We have Ameline. Surrender yourself to us at the southwest edge of the lawn, alone and unarmed, and she will go free. Deviate from this in any way, and I'll ensure you'll never find her.

It was signed with Ellbereth's name, and I wondered at her audacity until the paper flew out of my hands and into the fireplace.

Then my brain unstuck and I didn't give a crap about the details of her evil scheme.

Ellbereth had Ameline.

I could see the truth of that claim by Ameline's empty bed, and the weight of that knowledge sank cold fear deep into my bones.

Cold fear and hot anger.

I wanted to curse, to growl, to bellow my outrage. But I had to keep all my angst inside lest I wake Bryn. Because no matter what the note said, she wouldn't stay behind if she knew what I was about to do.

Dear, sweet Ameline whose warmth had been there when I needed it on every one of my darkest days.

Had they hurt her?

How had they managed to snatch her? I didn't believe for a second that Millicent would let them in. So she must have left our dorm, probably to visit the bathroom. I'd been banned from going alone—even in the middle of the night—but if Ellbereth and her cronies had been watching our door, they would've realized the same rule didn't apply to my roommates.

So they'd worked it to their advantage. Outsmarted us.

Because it had never occurred to me Ellbereth would stoop so low as to go for my friends.

It should have.

But—

I hauled my butt out of bed. Quietly. Trying not to wake Bryn. There was no point beating myself up about the things I'd failed to foresee. I had to go. Had to surrender myself. Because there was no way I would ever let Ameline die in my place.

And then maybe after I'd done that, I'd figure out a way of rescuing myself too.

I swallowed past my constricted throat, pulled on my shoes, and slipped out of our dorm room, leaving Bryn and Gus and most of my hope behind.

When I reached the designated meet point, no one was visible. I searched optimistically with my second sight, but the thread that linked a hollow to their life force was almost impossible to spot unless I could use their physical forms as a guidepost.

The night was black with only the slimmest crescent of a moon. I had not dared to bring a lantern in case they decided it counted as a weapon and therefore a breach of their instructions. So I waited, shivering in the darkness.

A minute passed. Two.

"Come on, you bastards," I muttered. "I'm alone and unarmed as ordered."

I assumed one of Ellbereth's gang was observing me from somewhere out there. And since walkers had better hearing than humans, I intended my words to carry.

Five more minutes passed before a figure emerged from the darkness. Wrapped as they were in a black cloak that blended with the gloom and hid their features, I didn't see them until they were almost upon me. I also couldn't see enough of their face to recognize the person inside.

It was probably designed to creep me out. Give them the power. But I was unafraid of the intangible, the imagined. The flesh and blood of the walkers and the very real devastation left by the Malus was nightmare enough.

The cloaked figure searched me for weapons. Thoroughly. It was just as well I'd resisted taking the dagger I routinely strapped beneath my pants leg, because they would've found it. They even had me remove my shoes and strip out of my cloak and uniform to put on a plain red sleeveless shift dress. The garment was not unlike a sack with a few extra holes cut in it.

Now I was freezing.

"Put this over your head," the hooded figure said in a voice of velvet masculinity.

It was a black cloth bag. Creepy as hell. And somehow having me do it myself made me feel more powerless than if he'd shoved it over my face.

The darkness of the night turned utterly black.

There was no need to bind my hands or drag me along with his magic. I was going willingly to the ritual that would render me dead or worthless. Since I couldn't see a damn thing though, he did have to guide me.

"Take my arm," he ordered.

And so in a parody of the gentlemanly gesture of the Before, he led me into the forest.

Though I was blind, my second sight lit up the world around me, and my bare feet relayed all sorts of information.

That was how I knew we were in the forest. The leaves squishy and damp beneath my toes. The life energy chaotic and bright. Plus I'd spent enough time there to be familiar with its sounds.

How easy it would've been for my escort to rid the world of me. To walk me into a terrant nest. Or the path of any predator and bind me for the few critical moments it would take for me to be devoured or torn apart.

They could claim I'd run away and fallen to the dangers of the wild. Everyone but my closest friends would believe it.

But Ellbereth, to her credit, really was trying to destroy my magic rather than me.

I wasn't feeling generous with credit though. Not after they'd snatched my best friend. Even if Ameline was released unscathed, she must be terrified right now. Every minute it took me to get there was another minute of suffering for her.

It did not take many more minutes.

My "gentleman" guide warned me of steps ahead. They were steep and hewn from soil according to my toes, and we descended into... something. The air filtering through the cloth over my face smelled of earth and little else. At the bottom of the stairs, the ground leveled out, but it was still bare soil beneath my feet.

There were two life forces visible in my second sight that I thought might be associated with Ellbereth's machinations. More than I expected to find given she and her friends were all hollows. The small griffin-shaped one must surely be Griff. The other, farther away and above us, was fuzzy but distinctly humanoid. A walker who hadn't undergone the ritual? But that couldn't be right... could it?

Someone's fingers brushed the nape of my neck. I flinched, but they only removed the black bag.

We were in some sort of underground chamber, the walls, floor, and ceiling all solid dirt except for the stairs I'd come down leading to the surface. Magical light illuminated the room, the brightness concentrated over a large slab table in the center.

But I noted all of this with only the barest of interest as my eyes desperately sought Ameline.

She was gagged and bound to the only other piece of furniture in the room, a simple wooden chair. Her face was grimy enough that I could see the tear tracks down her cheeks. But she was not harmed so far as I could tell. And Griff was nestled in her hair, tail swishing angrily but staying put on her shoulder.

Her expression only grew more worried when her gaze locked with mine. As if she'd hoped I wouldn't come.

I rushed to her—or tried—but two cloaked and hooded hollows blocked me.

"I'm here. Let her go," I demanded.

Ellbereth stepped between me and her cronies. Her hood was down, her flame-red hair looking dangerously wicked in this secret underground room. She tilted her head and smiled.

"Come now, you don't think we're so foolish as to release her before the ritual is complete, do you? We can't have her running for aid. But afterward, we will. Unharmed, I promise."

She patted the stone slab. "Lie down here, please."

There was no reason not to believe that Ellbereth would keep her promise, but I hesitated. There were four of them and two of us, assuming I could get Ameline untied. Those were crap odds, but they were only going to get worse once I lay down on that table.

Ameline shook her head, pleading with me not to go

through with it. She might be scared, she might've been brought to tears, but I knew she'd rather die than watch me sacrifice myself to save her.

Unluckily for Ameline, it was my choice to make.

Besides, this way there was a chance we both might live. Even if it was only a slim one.

My brain raced, trying to come up with a strategy that might get us out of here, our two gifts pitted against all of theirs. But I came up empty.

I met her eyes, trying to convey my peace with the decision. "I love you," I told her, not caring who else heard.

And then I lay down on the stone slab.

CHAPTER TWENTY-TWO

Ellbereth and her cronies tied me down with soft, silken ropes.

"This is going to hurt," she said, "but I *am* trying to help you. You have no grasp of how evil your magic is. It must be destroyed at any cost."

As much as I wanted to hate her, I could see by the fervor in her eyes that she believed it. Believed that it was better I endure agony and probable death than retain this wildcard magic.

And that scared me almost more than the cruel curved blade I'd noticed when I'd eased myself onto the table.

They finished tying me, my limbs spread-eagled across the slab in a most undignified fashion. But dignity was the least of my concerns.

Ellbereth checked each of my bonds herself, then raised her voice and announced, "She's secured."

That was when someone else came down the stairs, and a moment later, Healer Invermoore stepped into my field of view.

It was jarring to see her serene features and pristine white gown, usually in the light and airy beauty of the infirmary, here in this crude and grubby dugout.

She smiled gently at me, her clear gray eyes resting on my face, though not without a glance at my bonds first.

"Ellbereth's right, Nova. You have not seen nor tended to the thousands of warriors who have been wounded by the Malus. You have not witnessed what happens to those consumed by its devouring magic, so utterly emptied that their bodies disintegrate into dust mere days later, leaving nothing for their loved ones to say farewell to or lay to rest. No being should possess this power. It's unnatural. Unbalanced. And since walkerkind were responsible for bringing it about, it is our responsibility to undo it."

Shock and a sense of betrayal hit me like a fist to the gut. I'd always felt safe with the healer. I'd almost *liked* her.

But beneath the stunned betrayal was something worse. The unease, the doubt. What if Healer Invermoore and Ellbereth were right?

What if my magic was an abomination that should never have existed? What if I was not the Malus's downfall but its inroad onto this continent?

Certainly the number of people that were *for* my wildcard gift seemed markedly outmatched.

"You must know what I'm saying is true," Healer Invermoore continued softly, sympathetically. "Ameline came to me for supplies and advice that first night you were sick. Even your body senses the unnatural nature of this magic and tries to reject it."

When I didn't respond, didn't give her the agreement she seemed to be hoping for, Invermoore patted my tightly bound hand. "I will do all I can to ensure you survive the cleansing process."

There was something about the movement, her slight hesitation before touching me, that triggered something deep in my brain.

Healer Invermoore was not a hollow.

If I could break her skin, maybe even just scratch her with a fingernail, my magic would work on her. I could steal her life force and use that power to escape.

At the cost of her life.

As if Invermoore could see the thoughts on my face, she withdrew her hand. "It is my understanding that your magic is more limited than the Malus's. That you cannot take life force without first piercing the epidermal barrier. Is that correct?"

I could tell by the way she asked that she was already certain of the answer. She wanted me to know they were ready for anything I might try.

No wonder they'd searched me so thoroughly for

weapons and bound me so securely before she'd made her presence known.

Healer Invermoore picked up the curved ceremonial blade and made the first cut into my flesh. Pain and blood welled on my forearm. I supposed if magic was carried in our veins, it made sense they'd bleed it out of me.

Ellbereth and her minions began to chant. They'd shifted to stand around the table, one at each corner, and their harmonized voices lifted and fell in an unfamiliar cadence. An unfamiliar language. The sound was eerily beautiful, and the power of it made my hair stand on end.

Invermoore made another cut, parallel to the first and about an inch apart. More blood flowed. I gritted my teeth and watched the crimson liquid spill down my skin and onto the slab I was strapped to.

I knew then that if I wasn't prepared to make the healer bleed in return, if I wasn't prepared to take her life, there was no hope of escape.

Each new cut made me flinch involuntarily, but I did not cry out. Not yet. And my tightly constrained limbs could not recoil enough to ruin Invermoore's perfect precision. My skin might have been the canvas for a morbid work of art for all the care she took.

As the hollows continued to chant and my blood welled and flowed, I realized the slab had been created with this in mind. Gently sloped sides guided the liquid into channels that carried my blood away instead of letting it pool around my back.

How considerate of them.

Time seemed to speed up and yet slow down at the same time. My head spun, but whether from fear or blood loss or the magic in the room, I didn't know. A strange sort of lethargy was creeping over me.

I wasn't sure I cared.

I rolled my head—the one part of my body I was still free to move—to look at Ameline.

My friend's gaze was locked on me. Fear and horror and desperation shining there. And then, despite the gag, I heard her voice.

Stay strong and be ready. I'm going to try something.

I couldn't imagine what she thought she could do with her mindspeaking magic. Call in a beast from the forest to break us out of here? Any creature she might persuade to work with her would stand no chance against five walkers.

But whatever Ameline was trying, I didn't want to draw the walkers' attention to her. So I rolled my head back to study the earthen ceiling, the tree roots there sheared from whatever power had carved the underground space.

I tried to follow her instructions. To stay strong. To be ready. But the slim hope I'd had of escaping was draining away with my blood. To distract myself from *that* morose thought, I switched to my second sight.

There was only so much one could stare at a dirt ceiling after all.

The familiar abundance of life was dimmed by the quantity of soil between us, but I found it comforting somehow. Life would go on without me, whatever happened tonight.

A flurry of energy led me to two large and vibrant creatures circling a third. Obscured by earth and distance, the shape of their golden light was too hazy to identify them, but I could tell all three were big and powerful.

A growl ripped through the night, carrying down to our dugout and adding a discordant note to the melodic chanting. A spitting hiss sounded in response. And then the creatures' life forces flung themselves at each other, seeming to merge and separate and merge again.

I watched, mesmerized by the light show. Until a scream of pain carried to my ears and one of those light sources brightened.

Suddenly I understood Ameline's plan.

CHAPTER TWENTY-THREE

I reached out with my magic, uncertain if it would work across this distance, and *pulled* at the wounded creature's life force.

The resistance was strong, and in my weakened state, I worried I would lose this tug-of-war. But that thought resurrected the determination that had been slowly draining from me along with my lifeblood.

So I held on, pulled harder. The resistance gave way like a bursting dam.

Power flooded me. Healed me. Revived me.

Transformed me.

In four heartbeats, I wrenched free of my bonds, snatched the ceremonial blade from Healer Invermoore's hand, slashed through the ropes shackling Ameline to the chair, and pressed that same razor-edged blade against Invermoore's throat.

All before anyone could react.

My body was smeared with blood, but the pain and cuts were gone. I was sure I looked like a thing of nightmares as I bared my teeth.

"We are going to leave. You are going to let us. Or Healer Invermoore will be my next victim. And I don't think you'll like what I become with her power flowing through my veins."

In the breath that followed, Ameline rose on trembling legs, her eyes shining with an equal measure of hope and fear.

Ellbereth considered us for a moment. Then she waved a casual hand at Ameline, and my friend slammed back down in her chair.

"You might be fast and strong, but you forget there are five magic wielders in this room. Think about it, Nova. You might be right. You might even manage to kill a few of us and escape. But your friend here will die. I'll personally guarantee it."

She quirked a brow at me. "Unless you can raise the dead?"

I didn't answer, and she nodded as if this was expected. "Besides, if you murder even one of us, you will never graduate from the academy. Never face the Malus. So this power you foolishly believe may help the world, this power that has beguiled you, warped you already without your noticing, this power you are now considering sacrificing your friend and becoming a cold-blooded murderer to protect, will bring only that. Murder and death."

Her words held the ring of sincerity. Of truth.

Her truth.

But whether or not she was wrong about the rest, Ellbereth was right on one thing. I would not sacrifice Ameline to save my gift.

The tip of the ceremonial knife lowered a fraction as my supercharged body sagged in defeat.

"That's it," Ellbereth coaxed. "Return the blade to Invermoore and lie down on the table."

Don't.

That was Ameline. Abducted, gagged, and pinned to the chair by magic, yet still fighting.

Why is she bargaining with you? Why not magically force you to obey?

That was a good question.

You drew the life force of a stoneboar inside you. Use it.

A stoneboar. I hadn't realized that was what I'd drained. Would never have guessed it. Not because they weren't common enough but because of their single distinguishing trait.

There were three types of prey animals that flourished in the existing ecosystem. Those like rabbits and mosquitos that bred too fast to be wiped out. Those like the flum that had evolved inbuilt protective quirks that made them unappealing to predators. Or those like stoneboars, which were big, bad, and hard to kill. Stoneboars were especially hard to kill not only because they were the size of a rhino with hides tougher than inch-thick leather but because they had shields that made them impervious to all magic.

Except the Malus's.

Except mine.

Was it possible I now possessed that same shielding power? Why *hadn't* any of the walkers attacked me yet? Perhaps they were just being wary, unsure if my extra-strengthened limbs might push through any magic compulsion they could exert and fearing to risk Invermoore's life if it failed.

Or perhaps they couldn't cast anything on me.

Could I extend that protection to Ameline? There was nothing to lose by trying.

I focused on my friend, who was sitting rigidly on the chair, magic pinning her in place. And I visualized a barricade of transparent armored plates interlocking around her, one that would allow no magic through.

The rigidity of her muscles eased. Her eyes bored into mine in question. And I gave a slight nod.

She didn't stand. She was too smart for that, to give away our element of surprise. She just gave me a discreet thumbs-up.

And that was when I knew it was time to haul ass.

CHAPTER TWENTY-FOUR

I released my grip on Healer Invermoore, snatched up Ameline, and fled for the stairs.

The curved ceremonial blade would make a terrible close-combat or throwing weapon, but I kept it anyway. While I was pretty sure Ameline and I were immune to magical attack, we still had the physical to defend against.

I figured we had a few seconds head start before they came to terms with the fact that their magical attacks weren't working on either of us. Then they'd be out for blood. I caught sight of my crimson-smeared arm and amended that to *more blood*.

Lucky for us, amped up on life force, I was faster, stronger, and a better fighter than any walker.

I shoved Ameline out into the open air. "Run," I hissed. "I'll catch up."

Then I spun back to our tormentors to see if I might gain us some advantage.

There was little enough in the room to work with, and the walkers were already beginning to stir to physical action. With no time to devise a better plan, I dashed around the room and relieved them of as many weapons as I could carry.

I bounded up the stairs, flung my armful of stolen weapons into the care of a carnivorous tree, and dashed after my friend, already berating myself for not keeping one of the snatched swords.

My eyes could now see clearly in the darkness, and I caught up to Ameline with ease. She was flat-out sprinting, but it sure didn't feel like it. I placed my palm against her back and pressed gently to propel her to greater speeds, simultaneously glancing over my shoulder.

They were coming.

Four of the five were out of the hole now. And as a giant tree limb above us cracked and fell, I knew they'd figured out the flaw in our shield. Indirect magical attacks still worked fine.

I grabbed Ameline about the waist, raised her a few inches off the ground, and dashed forward to put the crashing limb between us and our pursuers.

It wasn't a comfortable way of carrying my friend, and I was considering putting her down, when brambles erupted at our feet. I threw her over my shoulder, ignoring her and Griff's shrieks of protest, and tore through the canes. The thorns ripped at my flesh, but the power flowing through me sealed the wounds seconds later.

Even so, I was gaining a better sense of my gift now, and I could feel the strain that took on my supply of stolen life force.

Dodge the nasties then. If I had to heal too much, I'd go through it too quickly. And if I ran out of juice, err, life force, we'd both be dead.

"Look out," Ameline cried, even as my ears picked up the sound of an arrow in flight. I dodged right. Into another patch of brambles, dammit, and sprinted on.

Guess I should've relieved them of their *long-range* weapons.

"They've stopped running," Ameline reported. "But I don't think they've given up. Something big is probably coming…"

Sure enough, the earth shook, threatening to turn my headlong flight into a headlong tumble into the dirt. No. Make that a ravine. The earth opened up, and I leaped just before the ground disappeared beneath my feet. I barely cleared it. And if my jump had fallen so much as an inch short, I was pretty sure that fissure would've slammed shut with me inside.

But the academy was just ahead now. I could see the comforting glow of Millicent's lights peeking through the trees. The dark shapes of the sentinel hedge cats guarding the threshold.

We dodged a final crashing tree limb, and then we

were past those hedge cats. But this time the thing that hunted me would not be stopped by their protective magic, so I kept running.

Millicent's doors sprung wide at my approach, and that small gesture made my eyes burn. Seconds later, I gladly gave her my blood to taste and fell through the doorway of our dorm. I knew Millicent would make the door disappear behind us in the outer hall, and only that made me lower Ameline to her own two feet.

She and Griff wore matching expressions of wind-blown and wide-eyed outrage. No, Griff's was outrage. Ameline's was a mixture of shock and relief.

"Gracious griffin's claws," she said. "That's some gift you've got there."

"How did you know I'd be able to use the stoneboar's abilities?" I demanded.

"I didn't. But I figured any energy you could draw on would help us, and life force is intertwined with magic, so I just hoped."

"But how did you get it to fight the other creatures? Isn't it impervious to your mindspeaking magic too?"

"Yes, but once I persuaded the pair of embercats to attack *it*, the stoneboar didn't have much of a choice in the matter."

"You're a genius."

"A genius who would've been utterly powerless without you."

"Funny, I was thinking the same thing." I pulled her into a hug. "Lucky we make a great team, hey?"

She half sobbed and half laughed, and I squeezed her tighter.

"We're in this together," I reminded her gently. That was the promise we'd made to each other over and over again as we were growing up. "Always."

Bryn chose that moment to join our conversation. Her short hair was mussed from sleep, her arms were crossed, and she was wearing a ferocious scowl.

"Together, you say? That begs the question of *what on earth did I just miss out on and why the hell didn't you bring me with you?*"

It was clear from the way she shouted the last part that she wasn't pleased about being left out.

Ameline hurried to explain. I chimed in on the parts she didn't know about.

Bryn's scowl stayed firmly in place.

"Problem?" I queried.

"I can't believe you let me sleep through all the excitement."

Um, *excitement?*

Our friend was officially bonkers. But I didn't think now was a good time to point that out to her.

"It's not like we had a choice," I pointed out instead.

Griff set to preening the feathers I'd disarranged in our mad scramble to safety, and Bryn's scowl deepened.

"Yeah well, you can't blame me for being upset. Even small-and-porky got to come along."

Now that the adrenaline was wearing off, Ameline was practically swaying on her feet. I felt no fatigue. Not yet. Stolen energy was still coursing through my system, but I decided to put an end to this conversation anyway so that my friends, at least, could get some sleep.

"Fine," I said. "I'm very sorry. The next time one of us gets kidnapped and the other is chosen to be carved up like a family roast and forced into an experimental ritual, we'll do everything we can to drag you into the disaster with us."

Bryn nodded as if this was a perfectly rational promise for me to make. "Good."

CHAPTER TWENTY-FIVE

I lay for a long time in the dark that wasn't dark to my energy-augmented eyes, listening to my companions' gentle snores. Wondering how I could protect myself and my friends.

Ameline and I had managed to outsmart Ellbereth and her minions this time. But what about the next? Or the time after that?

Sooner or later one of us was going to get killed.

And with Healer Invermoore on Team Ellbereth, a trip to the infirmary could prove just as dangerous as anything in the forest.

I wasn't a tattletale by nature, but if there was ever a time to get the authorities involved, this was it. I resolved to speak with Cricklewood after weapons training. Of all the professors, he'd seemed most invested in my wildcard magic. Dunraven, Wilverness, and the other professors tolerated it. Grimwort would happily see me dead. Hence, Cricklewood.

The other thing I thought about as the long minutes ticked by was the magic that was at the root of my trouble. To be fair, it had also gotten me *out* of trouble tonight, along with Ameline's quick thinking.

If our escape had taught me anything, it was that no one truly understood my magic. Including me.

I'd been told I had Malus magic, and I had swallowed that as fact. Even when experience suggested otherwise. But for all the similarities, my power was *not* the same as the Malus's.

The Malus drew from all living things. Every bug, leaf, creature, or fungus. And it didn't need to make them bleed first. Nor, I was beginning to suspect, did it have a problem with withdrawal like I did.

The Malus also had other abilities: taking over a creature's life force inside its body to use as a puppet and projecting fear so potent it could drive people insane.

But according to our lessons and every account I'd heard, one thing the Malus could *not* do was utilize the magic of those it drained.

Tonight, thanks to Ameline, I had done just that.

Which meant, despite the assumptions and accusations flung about, my gift was uncharted territory.

Hell, maybe I could do something other than kill.

The only way I would find out was to practice, experiment, and hunt down the answers myself. The sooner the better if I wanted to protect my friends and survive long enough to learn what I could really do.

So I vowed to ignore the voices in my head, telling me what was and wasn't possible, debating whether my power was evil or the key to victory, and the niggling fears that the Malus might somehow have a foothold in my mind or magic. I would shut them all out and begin practicing in earnest. Not just during Advanced Magic classes but before and after my other lessons too.

Then I would see what I could do about changing the world.

I was already dreading the withdrawals.

Weapons practice came and went. The stolen life force hadn't fully depleted yet, so I had to hold back to avoid hurting my sparring partners. It was about as challenging as swatting a trapped fly.

When the other students left for the next class, Ameline, Bryn, and I remained behind. Hopefully Cricklewood could give us some sort of note to preclude us from Dunraven's wrath at our delay. He hated students being late.

I might've come *before* weapons class except we all needed the extra sleep.

Cricklewood peered at us through narrowed eyes. "Did you have your brains eaten by worms and forget your way to class, or did you want something?"

"I need to talk to you," I said. "Privately."

He raised one scraggly white eyebrow and guided me to a small room tacked onto the outbuilding that stored the racks of special weapons.

I went in alone. If word got around that one of us had blabbed, I wanted the censure to fall on me.

Cricklewood followed me in and shut the door behind us. The room was small and cramped but surprisingly cozy. There were paintings on the walls, noncarnivorous plants in every available nook, and a desk piled with weapons in various states of repair instead of the usual papers. The chair Cricklewood seated himself in was plush and padded. The visitor's chair, on the other hand, was hard and compact with a backrest that dug in at all the wrong places. Doubtless to discourage visitors from overstaying their welcome.

I took the hint and got straight to the point, recounting what had been going on and why I was here.

The professor's wrinkles deepened as he listened, and he seemed to sag in his chair. When I was done, he rubbed his face with a hand as gnarled with age as any human's.

"I'm going to explain the situation to you," he said. "And you're not going to like it."

I waited.

"These are difficult times, and people are growing more difficult with them. Desperate even."

His eyebrows bristled at me as if making sure I was paying attention. I was.

"Some walkers strongly believe in this academy initiative. Most do not. The believers are the minority, but the majority have thus far bowed to their wishes because to do otherwise would cause a great deal of political backlash. Still, after thirty-seven years without result, tolerance among the majority is wearing thin. The only thing that's prevented the matter coming to a head before now is that the potential good of the academy initiative far outweighed the potential consequences."

His rheumy blue eyes fixed on mine.

"Until you, Nova. Your gift."

I swallowed, no longer sure I wanted to hear this. I'd assumed I was dealing with the professors and one fanatical student. What Cricklewood was insinuating was much larger and more complex.

He steepled his fingers on the desk as if collecting his thoughts.

"Your reaper magic is incredibly contentious. Some of those who support the academy initiative believe it might be what we've been waiting for. Almost everyone else wants the risk neutralized."

Have me killed, he meant. I was impressed the old coot could be so tactful when it suited him.

"It is not the professors at this academy deciding your fate. It's the members of the council. Two weeks ago, they *very reluctantly* acceded to the believers' wishes to wait and see how your gift develops. How *you* develop. But that ruling could be rescinded at any moment."

I'd known some of that already—that the concession to let me live was contingent on results. But I hadn't known those weighing that decision were a bunch of high-and-mighty walker council members I'd never so much as laid eyes on.

"To make matters worse," Cricklewood was saying, "Ellbereth's mother is the most influential council member alive today. It's possible, though I don't know this for sure and would deny ever saying so outside this room, that she is fully aware of what Ellbereth has been attempting to do. She could have even instructed her to do it. Certainly it wouldn't be the first time a member of the council has used their connections to achieve ends with minimal political fallout.

"As a hollow secluded away at this academy, Ellbereth is far enough removed from her mother to keep Lady Neryndrith's hands appearing clean, and Ellbereth's hollow status means she is protected from serious repercussions for all but the worst of offenses."

He didn't say it, but I understood taking a human life was not even close to being considered as *the worst of offenses.*

"So I could try talking to her. But it's your word against hers. And unfortunately for you, hers holds more weight with the people deciding your fate."

I slumped down in the hard seat. Fabulous. I'd had a feeling that was where the conversation was going.

"I don't give a crap about politics," Cricklewood said. "But my hands are effectively tied in this because if

I'm seen to aid you against a councilwoman's daughter without ironclad evidence of wrongdoing, the political uproar will harm rather than help you."

For a moment, just a moment, he looked truly apologetic.

I hadn't known the old professor could make that expression, let alone toward a student, and the vulnerability made me ask, "Are you a... believer?"

"More like an optimistic old fool." He rubbed his face again. "My partner was a hollow on the frontline back on our world, and the only reason I've bothered to outlive him for a hundred bleak and bitter years is because I want to see this war ended before I die. Jhaeros gave up his life for the cause, so I want to see it finished."

He frowned faintly at me.

"You give me hope that might still happen. Supposing you find a way of dealing with the more immediate problem."

In an eye blink, all trace of vulnerability vanished—so completely I would've thought I'd imagined it had it not been for the information he'd just shared.

The familiar cranky professor was back.

"And for the love of all that's good in the worlds," he growled, "don't kill Ellbereth. Otherwise, all hell will break loose."

He scowled at a spot above my head, making me curious as to his thoughts. "Did I use that idiom right?"

Oh. "Yes."

"Great. Now get your endangered backside out of my office before people start to wonder what we're talking about."

"Yes, sir." I pushed myself off the uncomfortable chair with a touch of relief, then paused. "Thank you."

Cricklewood nodded stiffly, and I turned for the door.

"By the way," he said, "that sword I made sure you were paired with, it cuts through magic. Might be useful."

I was still digesting that when the withdrawal hit me.

CHAPTER TWENTY-SIX

Six hours into my withdrawal, carrying myself and my sword to the bathroom felt like the hardest thing I'd ever done. I very nearly gave up halfway. But after all the sweating and vomiting, I *really* wanted a shower.

I also wanted to live to enjoy it.

So I pressed on.

Ameline and Bryn accompanied me. I felt bad about that, but anytime one of us left our dorm room, we were practically joined at the hip.

Ameline did offer to carry Gus on my behalf. But Gus told me he would accept no other wielder now. I suspected he was just enjoying watching me struggle, but then I also suspected that if Ellbereth tried again and the sword wasn't already in my hands, he wouldn't do me much good.

I still couldn't believe that it had been *Cricklewood*

who'd made sure I'd picked this particular sword. Perhaps Gus's claim that he'd been asleep was true.

When I reached the familiar bathroom tiles, I could've wept. I heroically resisted the urge to crawl, and careful to avoid dragging the tip of my heavy sword along those tiles, I made it at last into the shower stall.

Taking my clothes off presented another hurdle of monumental proportions, but I managed that too and turned on the taps.

The water was hot and cleansing and felt like magic.

I closed my eyes and reveled in it. The rivulets sluicing over my skin, washing away the sweat and other odors I didn't want to think about. The warmth soothing my tight and knotted muscles. And the blissful convenience of a nearby vomit receptacle if my stomach objected to this strenuous exercise.

I was just beginning to feel like life might be worth living when something tried to take it from me.

One moment I was standing there, letting the grime and aches drain away. The next, the stream of water jerked aside and some sort of metal collar snapped around my neck.

Too tight. I clawed uselessly at the unyielding garrote, unable to breathe. Some part of my brain registered it was the shower itself strangling me—the long brass arm that carried water up to the showerhead had leaped from its moorings on the wall and wrapped itself around my neck before becoming rigid brass again.

My frantic fingers scored my own flesh but did

nothing to the pipe. And in my panic, I was wasting precious seconds of oxygen. I pounded my fist against the side of the stall.

"Nova?" Came Ameline's hesitant voice. "Are you all right?"

But of course I couldn't answer.

My desperate, probably bulging eyes landed on Gus. The sword that could cut through magic, Cricklewood had said. I dove for it, but though *most* of the shower pipe had detached from the wall, the base was still secure and my metal collar pulled me up short.

If I'd had the breath to curse, I would've given Bryn a run for her money. Instead, I yanked at my leash, stretched my bare foot toward my sword, dragged it closer with my toes, and tried again.

There! My fingers wrapped around Gus's hilt, and I applied the last of the strength in my oxygen-depleted limbs to the awkward task of slashing at the tube of metal around my neck.

Somehow I managed to slice through the garrote without decapitating myself, and I collapsed to the floor in relief.

"Nova?" Ameline's voice was fraught with concern. "Answer me now or we're breaking down the door."

"Don't," I managed to say through a throat that ached with every blessed breath. I was lying against the tiles, naked and gasping, and the unwelcome puzzle pieces were falling into place.

By thwarting Ellbereth and her minions' plan to

drain me of my magic last night, I'd "forced" them to more extreme measures.

Ameline and I had defied the odds, my reaper gift giving me powers they'd been unable to fight in that underground chamber. Powers that had turned the tables and made *them* vulnerable, even with their numbers advantage.

From their perspective, it was easy to see how they'd conclude it was too difficult, too dangerous to complete the complex and lengthy magic-stripping ritual on me.

Killing me was a far simpler task.

After all, when not high on stolen life force, I was as helpless against them as a sitting duck.

Gus snorted in my mind. *A sitting duck with a magnificent sword maybe.*

CHAPTER TWENTY-SEVEN

I ended up recovering from withdrawal and the murder attempt just in time for the next "trust-building" trial. The irony wasn't lost on me.

If the professors wanted the students at the academy to learn to work as a trusting, cohesive unit, they really ought to start with the basics. Like prohibiting us from killing each other, for example.

Theus and Lirielle were standing outside our dorm room when Ameline, Bryn, and I emerged.

Theus looked us over with concern. "We heard about your... run-in with Ellbereth and thought you could use an escort to the arena. In case she hasn't given up yet."

My hand reflexively rose to my neck, the livid bruising mostly hidden by my shirt collar. She absolutely hadn't given up yet.

"Heard from who?" I asked.

Theus glanced down the empty passageway. "A certain professor."

Cricklewood then.

"Oh. Well, thanks."

A short, uneventful walk had us joining the other students assembled around the lake, which was in the process of draining. Ellbereth stared impassively at our arrival. If she was surprised to see me alive, I couldn't read it on her elegant face.

It was a face, I thought, that would look better with a broken nose. But that would only worsen the situation, so I tried for an equally impassive expression and was grateful for the comforting and restraining presence of my four companions.

Now we just had to get through this next arena challenge without sustaining an injury that might force us to the infirmary.

The lake finished draining, and Dunraven cleared his throat. "We'll be dividing you into groups of five."

The assembled professors walked among us to do just that, and I groaned inwardly when one of the conceited jerks from the first trial was assigned to mine. From his expression, tall, bright, and handsome number one hadn't forgiven me for upstaging him. But at least Lirielle was in my group too.

When everyone had been assigned a team, Dunraven said, "The setup is this: you're in the final throes of a long and difficult battle. A battle that you have, for all intents and purposes, lost."

A collective murmur ran through the students, and Cricklewood stomped his staff for order. "A scenario you combat virgins might want to get comfortable with."

Dunraven resumed his narrative. "Your magic has been depleted—which means any team member caught using it will be counted as a casualty." He paused to let that sink in.

"Most of your unit has already fallen, leaving your group of five as the only survivors. And two of you are so near to joining your fellow warriors in death that you will need carrying."

Cricklewood opened an ornate wooden box and held it up so everyone could see its contents. Two garnet-colored beetles the size and shape of a walnut lay against black fabric. They sparkled in the daylight like precious gemstones, and I thought they were jewelry until Cricklewood stroked one's back and it fluttered iridescent wings.

Animated or real?

Dunraven gestured at the display. "To help the theoretically injured teammates stick to their roles, they will be wearing a bloodjewel beetle pin, which will temporarily paralyze them from the neck down."

My eyes snapped back to the beetles. The decorative pieces were a far cry from the plain armbands that mirrored wounds from one wearer to another. I couldn't imagine the pretty red jewels had been made just for the academy and wasn't sure I wanted to know what they'd historically been used for.

I decided just to be grateful that none of my friends had been grouped with any of Ellbereth's. I didn't think she'd try anything in front of such a large audience— she'd gone to pains to keep her endeavors unwitnessed by any but those loyal to her. Still, I wouldn't have wanted to be teamed up with the murderous councilwoman's daughter and then rendered helpless by one of those beetle pins.

Had Cricklewood made sure that wouldn't happen?

"Your mission," Dunraven continued, "is to work together to conduct a strategic retreat without sacrificing any more lives. Between you and safety—in this case, the opposite side of the arena—is a stretch of land thick with Malus-possessed creatures."

Multiple heads turned in my direction at the mention of Malus possession. I held back a wince.

"If you have to leave your bloodjewel-wearing teammates behind, they'll be considered lost. If you have to use your magic, you'll be considered lost. And of course, if you take a life-threatening injury, you'll be considered lost and might even become so in actuality."

Fabulous.

But for all my personal issues and the skepticism that sprang from them, these trials were having an impact. Walkers and humans weren't becoming buddies, but they were starting to treat each other with something like respect.

With some notable exceptions anyway.

The group chosen to go first contained two of those exceptions. When Cricklewood joined them at the bottom of the arena to apply the beetle pins, I heard one of the walkers say, "Professor, the humans should be the wounded ones. They're weak, so they'd fall first."

"If they even make it as far as the battlefield," a second group member put in.

Cricklewood smiled. But it wasn't a nice smile. "Just for that, you two can be the paralyzed team members."

The two beetles flew from their nest of fabric and landed on the chests of their two targets. The walkers crumpled to the ground like boneless sacks of grain without so much as a hand to break their falls.

It did not stop them complaining.

That left two humans and one walker as the able-bodied members of the team. The humans didn't look any more thrilled about that than the walkers.

I didn't blame them. Especially as, after a quick discussion, the stronger of the two humans tried and failed to lift one of the paralyzed walkers off the ground. I'd never had to lift a walker myself, but I knew from lugging one of their bones around as a wand, ahem, a thaumaturgy rod, that they must weigh more than we did.

The single non-paralyzed walker, a girl with hair so black it was almost blue, assisted by hoisting the "injured" party up and slinging them over the human's shoulder. The kid, despite being fit and muscled from

Cricklewood's classes, staggered under the weight. His ability to fight while shouldering the burden would be almost nonexistent, but the third able-bodied teammate, a slight human girl, would have been a worse choice to carry the load.

The black-haired walker lifted the other "injured" teammate over her shoulder with relative ease, leaving her sword arm free.

And then every inch of the arena floor erupted.

A multitude of animated enemies made of stone and wood and dirt poured from the earth. Their forms were too many to catalog and their numbers too numerous to count. Animals, large and small, real and mythical, humanoid figures wielding crude but effective weapons hewn from the same materials they were, and the occasional flying creature as well.

They were smaller than the golems from the first trial but infinitely more abundant. And as I watched, the struggling team all but disappeared under the seething mass of adversaries.

Somehow the team managed to fight their way forward, slashing and hacking in frenzied concentration. It was probably hard *not* to hit something.

But they were only a quarter of the way across when their momentum slowed. Stopped. Hemmed in by too many enemies and not enough fighters.

The unencumbered human girl seemed to be putting in a heroic effort, but her staff, while good for keeping the foes out of striking distance, failed to fell them fast enough. The black-haired walker was swift and skilled but hindered by her efforts to protect the guy slung over her shoulder. And the guy carrying the second walker tried to lend what assistance he could whenever one of them came close to being overwhelmed, but that help was limited.

I didn't see what happened. Not exactly. Perhaps one of the enemies got clever and yanked the staff out of the human girl's hands. Perhaps as she tired, one of them finally slipped through her defense and she was unable to stop the torrent of creatures that followed. But suddenly someone was screaming and then a blast of magic sent every animated monster stumbling back.

It didn't stop the screaming though.

A moment later, the enemies fell where they stood, much as the beetle-wearing walkers had. Someone among the professors must have decided it had gone far enough.

But that didn't stop the screaming either.

Then one of the walkers who'd been wearing a bloodjewel pin was being carried past me on his way to the infirmary. They passed close enough that I could see the large bite out of his side. So large that several of his ribs and the pinks and dark reds of his organs were visible.

The girl who'd been wielding the staff followed, pale-faced and nursing her arm like it might've been broken.

The remaining three were shaken but okay. They

wiped sweat from their faces and settled down to watch the next unfortunate team.

Cricklewood's beetles had flown back to him at some point, and when his eyes landed on me, I knew.

He crooked a finger at us. "You're up next."

CHAPTER TWENTY-EIGHT

I wanted to swallow, but my mouth was feeling awfully dry right then.

We trudged down into the arena. Well, *I* trudged. Lirielle had a floaty sort of spring in her step that suggested she was en route to a night of merrymaking rather than battle.

Tall, bright, and handsome, whose ugly sneer made me want to change his nickname, doubtless would've preferred the two humans of our group to be paralyzed, but after what happened with the first team, he was wise enough not to voice his opinion.

We waited with bated breath for Cricklewood to choose.

The bloodjewel beetles, which were exquisite up close, flew to Dexter and Luthien. One human, one walker. Both large, heavy males.

That left me, Lirielle, and Sneer Face to carry the

"wounded" and fight our way across the arena. Sixty yards had never seemed so far.

Sneer Face shouldered the paralyzed walker and turned to Lirielle. "Looks like you and I will have to take on the burden since the human can barely lift her sword without the stolen life force of others.

"Fine with me," Lirielle said. "I prefer to be challenged than bored."

My head whipped in her direction. I'd spent quite a lot of time with Lirielle recently—in addition to protecting my back in the forest every day, she and Theus had taken to joining us for the occasional meal. So I was accustomed to her quirks. While she was with us in body and vaguely aware of what was going on in her immediate surroundings, the larger part of her mind was usually soaring elsewhere along paths unknown. Except now, she sounded so... well, *present.*

"Back to back to back," she ordered, scooping up the human male with an ease that should've been impossible with her slender frame. A naked sword gleamed in her hand, and there was a second sheathed at her waist.

I tore my eyes from Lirielle to the goal on the far side of the arena. "Why don't we travel along the wall so we only need to defend on one front?"

Lirielle canted her head. "Because along the wall is near twice the distance, and with three of us fighting, our ability to swing a sword will be severely hampered by the risk of hitting an ally."

Both were good points, but I didn't get a chance to

tell her so because right then the disassembled army erupted into menacing life.

We put our backs together, each of us forming one point of a defensive triangle formation. I took the lead point. Unencumbered, it made sense to put me on path-clearing duty.

Or so I thought until I saw Lirielle fight. I'd watched her in other trials and marveled at her skill with both one and two blades. But it was a whole new level of amazing to experience it at close quarters. If I hadn't been so busy holding up my own section of the defense, I would've loved to gawk.

Gus did one of his sighs. *Yes. I don't know why* she *couldn't have become my wielder.*

"Oh please," I muttered. "You would hate having to share the glory with a second sword."

He harrumphed but didn't gainsay me.

The sheer mass of creatures jostling to kill us was almost overwhelming. Everything from large bears or mythological monsters to floppy clay-eared rabbits, vicious raccoons and the occasional humanoid or goblin. Some bore crude weapons like clubs or axes made from extensions of themselves. Others used claws or horns or tusks or teeth to rip and render flesh.

All of them were out for our blood.

But in their disorganized, crowded frenzy, they bumped and shoved and impeded each other's attacks —making them easy targets for my blade. And perhaps due to Gus's ability to slice through magic, they fell to his wicked black edge like wheat before a scythe.

Our adversaries were poor fighters with crude weapons, but in a numbers game like this one, they'd win out eventually. There would be no doubt of the outcome in a real battle.

But we didn't need to kill them all. We just needed to reach the other side of the arena.

So I slashed and parried and occasionally dodged, careful not to leave an opening that an ambitious clay creature could use to attack my companions' backs. We pushed onward, gaining ground slowly but surely with relentless intent. And though I could feel myself tiring, I started to think we might make it.

We were halfway across the arena when our plan went to hell.

Sneer Face staggered against my side. "Stars and suns," he cursed. "I lost my sword. We need to get it back."

In my peripheral vision, I saw Lirielle flick a glance over her shoulder while simultaneously decapitating her nearest foe. "Your arm's broken. How are you going to wield it?"

"I'll figure something out. Just help me, dammit."

Sneer Face kicked a rocky rodent into the face of an oncoming humanoid, and I cut down the club-wielding gorilla thing that rushed into the small opening that provided. I barely spun in time to meet the next opponent.

Getting his sword was easier said than done. It would be a miracle if we could find the blade under the piles of bodies—or more accurately, piles of rubble —around us.

"How are you at fighting left-handed?" I dared to inquire while slamming Gus into the chest of a large hunting cat that had shoved the other opponents aside. I wasn't about to risk our necks to retrieve a weapon he could barely use.

"Fine."

"Crap," Lirielle countered.

She would know since she could fight equally well with a sword in each hand. Though right now she was using only one of her blades since the human draped over her shoulder limited the motion on that side of her body.

"Why not borrow Lirielle's spare?" I suggested.

"No!" Lirielle and Sneer Face shouted at once.

"Then forget about your sword," I said. "Take the injured guy from Lirielle so she's free to fight with both hands."

"No way," he snarled. "Then I'll be completely defenseless. I'm not trusting my life to a human brat!"

Lirielle's sword made a sweeping arc in the edge of my vision, and two more stone creatures crumpled. "A human brat who's outdone you at every challenge since the transformation," she pointed out.

"Only because she's not pulling her fair share of the weight by carrying anyone right now."

Lirielle cut down a wolf that was racing at Sneer Face while I caught an eagle in the gut. "Neither are you since you dropped your weapon," she retorted. "Stop arguing with reason and take Dexter already. If one of us fails to protect you, you can always defend yourself with magic."

Muttering and whining about how well that turned out for the first team, Sneer Face conceded. And at last we were able to resume our slow progress across the arena.

My skin was slick with sweat and dirt turned to mud, and the fighting was so fierce I hadn't dared block my vision for the split second it would take me to wipe my brow. But Gus was brilliant, and Lirielle even more so. (Not that I'd share that comparison with my pointy companion if I could help it.)

She was a whirlwind of wicked edges and moved so fast I wasn't convinced I could best her even if I'd been powered by additional life force. Trying to defend a wider angle meant I could see less of Lirielle now, but I didn't miss the number of occasions one of her flashing swords encroached into my territory to save my ass whenever I risked being inundated.

By Gus's and Lirielle's skill and my sheer determination, we made it across the arena.

Sneer Face bore our two paralyzed teammates roughly to the ground and strode off to find his sword (and then probably the infirmary) without a backward glance.

Lirielle shot me a triumphant grin not in the least bit dimmed by the mud and dust spattering her face.

"It was a pleasure to fight by your side, Wildcard."

Then she sheathed her swords, and I could see her mind already untethering itself from the material world as she drifted up the stairs.

Bemused but smiling, I trailed after her.

In the end, we were one of only three groups to reach the far side of the arena with every team member "alive."

But my friends made it out healthy and whole, and that was all I cared about.

CHAPTER TWENTY-NINE

If someone had told me a few months ago that a snail infestation would radically change my life, I'd have backed away slowly and then avoided that person ever after.

Yet that's exactly what happened. The snail revolution thing, that is. Not somebody predicting it.

I was eating breakfast when Glenn and Glennys came into the dining hall, muttering about the damage a magical snail infestation was wreaking on their roses.

In a flash of inspiration, I promised them I'd take care of it. And when the time came for Grimwort's Advanced Magic lesson, I set to work.

One snail at a time.

I didn't regret draining the snails of their life force. Heck, I was even doing community service at the same time. Though I did feel bad about scraping their gelatinous gummy sides with a needle first.

Theus, green eyes sparkling, watched on with great amusement while Lirielle spent most of the hour far away in her own dreamy preoccupations. But they were guarding my back, so I limited my protests to an occasional half-hearted glower in Theus's direction.

It only made his smile deepen.

Still, the slimy, gloopy mollusks were perfect for practicing my magic on. Draining their tiny life forces required finesse and allowed me to experiment for longer periods and multiple drawings without risk of becoming overly supercharged. That in turn meant I didn't wind up with anything worse than minor nausea during withdrawal.

Even better, this particular variety possessed a tiny amount of magic of their own. Unlike most snails, they could exude slime from every part of their body and used the slime's vaguely magical properties to taste foul to natural predators as well as protect themselves from poisons absorbed through the skin and shell.

It wasn't the most useful magic ability for me to steal —and I wasn't stoked about exuding snail goo from my own skin—but I could still practice the mechanics of stealing and wielding it. Plus it convinced Gus to refrain from his scathing commentary on occasion when I threatened to gum up his hilt with slime.

After each day's official lessons were done, Ameline and Bryn relieved Theus and Lirielle of their Nova-sitting duties.

Bryn was itching for Ellbereth to try something so she could vent some of her fiery displeasure, but as the sky darkened and other students took time for recreation or extra sleep, the academy grounds were empty except for us and Cricklewood or Glenn and Glennys occasionally passing by. So Bryn made do with juggling fireballs and keeping us all warm in the winter evening chill. Sometimes Ameline would encourage Griff, whose feathers were becoming less scraggly and who was getting better at flying every day now, to fly through Bryn's fireballs like an obstacle course or hunt down his own food. He turned his nose up at the foul-tasting snails, preferring instead to prey on the juicy moths and tiny bats that came out after dark.

Bryn's prowess with fire made my own magic practice with the snails even more laughable, but I persisted anyway.

And it was on my sixth day of doing this when the population was wearing thin that I learned something very interesting about my wildcard gift.

Worried about running out of snail victims, I tried to finesse my skills to an even greater extent and take just a fraction of the life force from one snail. To my shock, it worked. And further, the snail I'd pinched that smidgen of life force from continued oozing itself around Glenn and Glennys's rosebush, munching as it went.

Hardly able to believe it, I marked the snail with indigo ink, much to my friends' amusement. And the next morning it was not only alive, but its life force was as bright as the rest of them again.

"Don't you get it?" I demanded of Bryn and Ameline, whom I'd dragged out before breakfast to check on my snail friend. "This means I can take and use life force and magic *without* killing the creature I steal it from. Without even causing it any lasting harm."

My friends stopped teasing me about my snail experimentation after that.

Mostly.

CHAPTER THIRTY

Snail practice aside, the attempts on my life didn't stop after the shower incident. One day as I stood at the arena's edge to watch the team inside, a freak gust of wind nearly sent me tumbling over the sheer drop to the unforgiving ground below. Only Lirielle's lightning-fast reflexes, reaching out to grab my belt, prevented it from working.

Another day during breakfast, a chunk of bread lodged in my airway and refused to move no matter how I coughed or spluttered. Bryn saved me that time by setting fire to the table Ellbereth and her friends were seated around, and suddenly the bread came up just fine.

On a third occasion, we were passing through one of the grand chambers when the large chandelier that graced its lofty ceiling smashed to the floor. Millicent reacted faster than we did, yanking the rug we were walking on and us with it out of harm's way.

It was fortunate Ellbereth didn't want my death linked back to her because it placed far more constraints on her than we could have. She stuck to things that might be construed as accidents in public, and we took special care whenever we were away from the other students.

Gus's ability to cut through magic saved my butt on more than one occasion. For all that his milk-and-honey obsession was annoying, I was more grateful than ever he was immune to rust because I insisted on having him within easy reach whenever I showered.

Our dorm room became a refuge for us all, though even there I kept Gus near.

And so my days became an exhausting cycle of learning about my magic and trying not to die.

In addition to classes and arena trials of course.

It was a mixture of luck, my sword, and the loyalty of my friends (because somewhere over the past weeks, I *had* uneasily come to count Theus and Lirielle among that number) that I was still alive. And I was beginning to realize that sooner or later that luck would turn on me.

Each day, I was growing less and less confident that I would survive long enough to pit my wildcard gift against the Malus.

But it was during the night that I should've been afraid.

Flashing lights roused me from sleep. But before I could so much as open my eyes, my mattress—or to be more precise, Millicent—flung me across the room.

Which turned out to be just as well because two paralyzing bloodjewel beetles flew through a hole in the ceiling directly above my bed. A hole that hadn't been there when I'd fallen asleep.

I scrambled for my sword, shouting a warning to Bryn and Ameline.

But I was too slow on both fronts.

The nearest beetle stabbed me in the chest, and my limbs went dead, toppling me to the floor on top of the sword I'd been trying to grab. My neck still worked, and I craned it in time to see the second beetle fell Ameline in a similar fashion. Except she hadn't made it all the way out of bed yet, so at least her landing was soft.

I remembered from the arena that we could still use our magic despite the paralysis, but that did me zero favors since the only borrowed magic ability I had in my system was snail slime. A quick check confirmed there was nothing conveniently bleeding in our vicinity.

Ameline's communication magic wasn't going to help either. Griff wasn't even in the dorm room because with his plumage and fur grown in to protect him from the cold, he'd taken to going on late-night jaunts when the mood struck him.

And our attackers weren't done yet.

I rolled my head the other way to see that four walkers had dropped through the hole in the seconds it had taken to neutralize Ameline and me. My blood ran cold.

Ellbereth and some of her minions. And I was helpless. Magnificent sword or no.

Gus, pressed beneath my unresponsive limbs, for once did not contradict me.

But Bryn wasn't done yet either. She welcomed the intruders with a barrage of fireballs. Unfortunately the overly organized walkers were prepared for this contingency, sporting magical shields that flickered but did not fall under the ferocious attack.

That didn't stop Bryn from trying. The fiery assault intensified until there was so much fire in the air it seemed impossible that the entire room hadn't caught alight. Yet Ameline, Millicent, and I were all unscathed, and I still had enough oxygen to breathe. It was freaking impressive.

A spot on my chest heated, and I realized Bryn was simultaneously trying to burn the beetle pin. But while the fabric beneath it began to smoke, the bloodjewel itself did not alter. Nor did my inability to move.

Damn.

No matter how gifted she was with fire, Bryn didn't stand a chance against the four powerful and prepared walkers. I watched uselessly as they pushed forward, protected by their magic shield. When they drew nearer to Bryn and she failed to draw her axe or dodge away, I realized they must be physically restraining her with magic too.

One of the walkers hit her on the head. Hard. And the fires flickered out.

Hell's hot sulfurous breath. If they'd done her any permanent damage—

They released their magical hold and Bryn fell to the floor.

Then they came for me.

I was certain I was about to die. Instead, they gagged me with something that tasted of mint and dirt and then the same stupid black bag they'd used before was shoved over my head.

Were they going to attempt the ritual again?

If so, there would be no escape. Not this time. Even if animals happened to fight nearby, allowing me to draw on their life force without Ameline orchestrating it, paralyzed as I was, my magic would do little good.

I could rally no resistance, could do nothing but flop limply about, when they picked me up. I cursed them through my gag, but it came out too muffled to offer any satisfaction. All I could do was pray they would leave my friends alive.

Unseen hands hoisted me over a shoulder, and then I was lifted and passed to another set of hands that hauled me through the hole in the ceiling.

No one spoke as they carried me. I knew from the change of temperature and the chill breeze against my skin that we had traveled outside.

Unable to move more than my head, unable to

shout through the gag, unable to see a damn thing, all I could do was imagine how my life would end.

My eyes stung, but I refused to give them the gratification of seeing any tears. If they bothered to remove the bag over my head before they killed me. Perhaps I wouldn't even see it coming.

And then the person whose shoulder I was riding on shifted their gait. Like they were walking down a series of steps. But it couldn't have been the underground room in the forest. We hadn't traveled far enough for that. So—

I was lowered to the ground with a gentleness that seemed incongruent when they were about to kill me, and then the bag around my head was removed.

Ellbereth's pale face loomed in the dark. "I'm sorry it has to end this way." The apology seemed as genuine as it could be under the circumstances. Though now I knew her mother was a politician, I was more suspicious of her apparent sincerity. "If only you'd cooperated and let us cleanse you of the evil magic. I didn't want to... Well, I suppose there's no point lamenting over what might have been."

She was remarkably civil for a murderer.

"You're in the arena," she told me as her minions carried over two of the giant weapons from the wall.

Really? This was how it was all going to end? Chopped in half by a rusted battle-axe or great sword?

But Ellbereth had not been "civil" enough to remove

my gag, so I couldn't voice my questions aloud. Not understandably anyway.

To my surprise, the walkers laid the weapons across my torso, careful to avoid dislodging the beetle. The weight was cold and uncomfortably heavy on my paralyzed body.

But still better than being cleaved in two, I supposed. My brain scrambled to make sense of the odd gesture.

"We're going to leave, and then the lake is going to refill. I've heard drowning isn't a pleasant death. But at least it will be over quickly. And this way everyone— well, everyone that matters—will believe it was an accident."

Ellbereth paused, a smile crooking her lips.

"Silly of you to go swimming alone in the middle of the night."

She turned to her companions. "Let's go. We'll put the blood jewels and weapons back when it's done."

And then she and her minions disappeared into the darkness, leaving me to drown.

CHAPTER THIRTY-ONE

Frigid water seeped up from the soil beneath me, dampening the back of my paralyzed body and unbound hair. I allowed a few tears to fall then. Curse Ellbereth and her cronies, this wasn't how I was supposed to die. So uselessly. Futilely. Fruitlessly.

But what the hell could I do? The bloodjewel beetle was impossible to reach with my teeth, and the heavy weapons pressing me to the sand would ensure I had no hope of floating.

Think, Nova. Think!

I couldn't move. I checked and failed once again to find any convenient life forces to steal from. And my only current magical ability was to ooze snail slime.

The water rose, trickling into my ears, and the world went quiet.

But I realized then that the snail slime might not be so useless after all.

I concentrated on the spot where the bloodjewel pin stabbed into my chest and magically conjured up some slippery, goopy, viscous slime to ooze from my skin. The pin shifted a fraction.

The water was rising faster now, gaining momentum. I sucked down one final breath.

The lake covered my mouth and spilled up my nostrils.

I oozed more slime. Pouring every desperate ounce of energy toward it. And the pin slipped a little more. The rising water helped rather than hampered in this respect at least, making the pin lighter, easier to shift.

It also chilled my body, my blood, my unresponsive limbs.

My world grew darker as more and more inches of water blocked out the stars above. But I was so close now. If I could just dislodge the pin, I could swim to the surface and drag in as much oxygen as my body wanted.

Hell, I could possibly just stand up.

But whether an inch or a mile, the distance to the surface made no difference to my aching lungs. Both would prove lethal. I'd been holding my breath, willing my body to subtract as much oxygen from that single, final lungful as it could, but instinct was demanding I release it. Take a fresh breath. Now.

A trickle of bubbles escaped my lips before I clamped them shut again.

I was running low on slime-oozing ability. It had taken the partial life force of a *lot* of snails to give me that much, but if I'd realized it might make the difference over whether I lived or died, I would've taken more. Too late now. I scraped the measly dregs of the magic together for one last push and prayed it would be enough.

I could no longer see the beetle pin in the growing darkness, but I felt it move. A tingling sensation surged through my limbs, and then, thank the heavens, they responded at last to my brain's frantic commands.

I shoved the heavy weapons aside and launched myself off the bottom of the lake. Oxygen, here I come!

The lake had risen higher than I'd thought—or maybe my body was weaker than I realized—but the lightening gloom assured me I was nearing the surface. I released another stream of bubbles from my cramping lungs and kicked my heavy legs. Soon, any moment, I would crest the top of the water and suck down a heavenly breath of fresh air. My eyes were locked on the increasingly visible stars in promise.

Then the stars disappeared. Obscured by the crystalline fragments of water beginning to freeze. Quickly transforming into the pure white of solid ice.

My hands hit the frozen wall, instinctively recoiling from the stinging cold. But I forced them to pound at it, claw at it with everything I had left.

The ice was unyielding. Merciless.

Even fueled by adrenaline and desperation, my body was growing sluggish. Slow to respond to my commands. There might have been irony in there somewhere.

I let myself sink, just a little. Searching for a gap in the ever-expanding ice. There!

I swam for it. My strokes clumsy as my heavy, numb, oxygen-starved limbs struggled to obey. But even before I reached that gap, that promise of air, of life, the ice closed over.

The last of my breath rushed from my lungs in a mixture of fear and frustration. Of failure. Of defeat.

Breathe my body told me. Demanded. But I kept my lips clamped tight, knowing that way offered no relief.

No relief except death.

My lungs empty and my limbs once again unresponsive, I sank. Down. Away from the ice.

And I thought of lovely and loyal Ameline paralyzed in her bed, unaware I was about to break our childhood promise. Of Bryn lying where she'd fallen, her daring defeated and fire quenched. I even thought of Lirielle's flashing blades and faraway daydreams. Of Theus's deep forest-green eyes I'd believed too dangerous to venture into. And then I thought of my family. Mila's chubby cheeks that only became more so when she smiled. Reuben's half-hearted scowl failing to conceal his tender heart. My mother's hardworking hands and the way she softened when Mila or Reuben crawled into her lap. My father's bear hugs that had always made me feel safe.

Breathe my body demanded again. My vision was spotted with black. My head was dizzy, muddled, and my thoughts slipped from me until it was empty of all but dark, icy sludge.

I gave in to instinct.

Water flooded up my nose and down my lungs. It burned. Stinging with the fury of a hornets' nest. A fury I was no longer able to muster.

Tears of pain leaked from my eyes. Then my world turned truly black, and my mind dissolved into the darkness.

CHAPTER THIRTY-TWO

My body hurt too much not to be alive.

My torso spasmed as I heaved up water. Then almost drowned on it again until someone rolled me over. On my side, the water had somewhere else to go, and I retched up more of it. A lot more of it.

My throat, lungs, nasal passages, and stomach burned like I'd downed liquid fire instead of simple lake water.

Note to self, don't do that again.

More spasms wracked my body until the coughing and retching no longer brought up any liquid. Then I turned my attention to breathing, sucking down lungful after lungful of delicious air. It made the burning worse, but I didn't care.

My head pounded and my entire body felt like a giant had picked me up and wrung me out like a dishcloth.

But I was alive. Somehow.

How?

I forced my eyes to open, even though the feeble starlight hurt them too.

Theus was kneeling over me. His handsome face was pinched with worry, but that changed when he spotted me looking back at him.

"Thank the stars," he breathed. And the glad warmth that suffused his face rendered me mute.

Perhaps in contrast to that warmth, or perhaps because my brain was finally getting the air it needed to function, I began to shiver violently. We were in the last clutches of winter, and I was soaked head to toe in icy water. No wonder I was freezing. But I still wanted to know how I was even alive to feel so miserable.

"How?" I managed to croak through my numb lips and burning throat.

Theus frowned at my shuddering, and the air around me heated, causing my wet clothes and hair to steam.

"Ameline's griffin friend fetched me," he said. "Millicent let him in to harass me in the middle of the night, so I knew something must be urgently wrong. He led me to the lake. I saw the ice and knew it wasn't cold enough for it to have formed naturally, but I couldn't see past it. So I started the lake emptying and melted as much of the ice as I could while it drained. Then I saw you. At the bottom. Lifeless."

He swallowed. Like the memory or the retelling of it

was difficult. Then he tentatively wiped a tangle of wet, steaming hair out of my face.

I hadn't even noticed it was annoying me until he shifted it. Had it been annoying him too? Or—

"I'm going to do some basic healing on you now, is that okay? I'm nowhere near as good as Healer Invermoore, but I understand it's not safe for you to visit the infirmary."

Lungful after lungful of blessed air and the heat provided by Theus were doing me good, and I struggled to sit up, forcing my exhausted abdomen to hold me upright.

"I'm fine," I lied.

I wasn't. Not really. My body would heal well enough if I gave it time. I was less sure about my mind or my future. But right then I was more worried for my friends.

"We need to get to Bryn. They hit her head hard enough to knock her out."

Speaking felt like sawing at my vocal cords with a blunted blade, and even sitting up felt precarious. My head protested the exertion by arming someone with a hammer and letting them go to town on my skull.

Theus shook his own head. "We'll get to your friends faster if you can stand on your own and walk at a decent pace."

I wasn't sure that was true. Not technically, since he could carry me easily enough. But I'd been carried to my near execution like a sack of potatoes. I wanted to walk away from it.

So I nodded, not wasting words on vocal capitulation.

Theus laid a hand above my heart, and his magic flowed through me like the spreading warmth of sunshine on a cold winter's day. Soothing the pain in my throat and airways, dulling the stinging, blistered rawness to something like a mild case of the flu. Quieting the pounding in my temples and making my brain feel… well, less waterlogged. And sending warmth and energy into my exhausted, aching muscles.

"That's all I can manage with your life force as low as it is," he apologized as if he hadn't just made me feel a hundred times better. Then one corner of his mouth lifted. "But I'll stalk down some snails in the forest for you as soon as we've checked on Bryn and Ameline."

Griff—who was sitting on Theus's shoulder, something I'd failed to notice in the prior haze of pain—flapped his wings at hearing Ameline's name.

I cracked a smile and took the hand Theus offered to help me to my feet.

"Thank you."

Maybe I held on a moment longer than necessary, but I was too exhausted to chide myself for it.

Bryn was okay except for a mild concussion and a nasty

lump that Theus took care of. I was so relieved my knees went weak. Or maybe my knees were already weak.

Ameline was unharmed. The first thing she did after we removed that cursed bloodjewel beetle was wrap me in a hug. Then she offered her shoulder for Griff to land on and scratched him in all his favorite places.

There was no sign of the hole in our ceiling.

But for all that we'd escaped without permanent injury, the mood was somber. Especially as I relayed what they'd done to me. How close I'd come to dying.

"They're not going to stop until you're dead," Bryn said, uncharacteristically grim.

I'd known that, known it for weeks, but it hadn't seemed real, not entirely. Hadn't held the same weight as it did now. The weight of terror and hopelessness I'd experienced under that ice. The weight of knowing in my last moments that I'd ultimately done so little to help those I loved. Not when the world would be ending in ten short years.

"I know," I said simply. But my hands curled into fists at my sides.

Perhaps I should accept that reality. Bow to the inevitable. At least that way I might be able to stop my friends from becoming collateral damage. But the fury I thought had drowned with me was back, and everything in me wanted to fight.

I just didn't know how.

Tears welled in Ameline's eyes, but she didn't let

them spill. "They can't. This isn't how it's going to end. We'll come up with a way to stop them."

But she trailed off, as empty of ideas as I was.

Bryn was staring into the fireplace, the dwindling flames and her own stillness testaments of her distress. "You all saw how much use my fire was against a well-planned attack."

"More use than my magic," I pointed out.

We sat in our shared misery, mulling over the facts. We had several months of training left to complete before we would be divided into warrior units and sent to the Malus war front. Several months in which Ellbereth and her minions would continue to escalate their attacks. Growing bolder, more cunning, and perhaps more ruthless too.

And if we failed to come up with an ingenious plan to thwart them, I would not survive till graduation.

We sat in hopeless silence.

Theus cleared his throat.

"I might know of a way you could get Ellbereth to call off her attacks," he offered hesitantly. "But it would involve breaking an awful lot of rules and may well place you in as much danger as it saves you from. Let me sleep on it."

CHAPTER THIRTY-THREE

We all tried to sleep. Some of us more successfully than others. Exhaustion from my near drowning claimed me quickly, but my rest was plagued with nightmares. Not of my own death, but that of my friends, my family, and the entire world.

So when someone knocked lightly on our dorm room wall before sunrise, I staggered out of bed to see who it was. Millicent anticipated my need and obligingly made a peephole for me.

Theus. The man who'd dragged me out of a frozen lake. His hair was rumpled with sleep, his clear-cut jaw sported a layer of stubble, and his handsome face was unusually drawn.

What was he considering risking to save me?

I opened the door that was still visible on our side of the wall.

"I will help you," he said, his voice pitched not to

carry. "But we cannot speak on academy grounds. Will you come with me?"

"Of course. I'll wake the others."

"No. Don't. Please. Revealing this information to you is betrayal enough to my own kind."

"Oh." I hesitated, but Theus had saved me time and time again. Whatever his intentions were, I need not fear for my life with him. "Give me a minute to get ready."

I wrote a note on the largest sheet of paper I could find to prevent Ameline and Bryn from freaking out, and ended it with an inside joke so they'd know I hadn't penned it under duress. Then I pulled on my boots and cloak, strapped on Gus and my hidden dagger, and joined Theus in the hallway.

We walked in silence through Millicent's corridors and out one of the less used side doors.

Outside, the air was cold and damp, and I pulled my cloak tighter around me. We tramped across the frost-laden grass, our breath sending clouds of condensation before us. The sight of the lake glinting in the waning starlight elicited a shudder that had nothing to do with the temperature. Its smooth surface was unblemished by wind, deceptively tranquil.

I couldn't imagine choosing to swim anytime soon. Maybe ever again.

Maintaining our silence, we stepped past the sentinel hedge cats into the forest, and I was grateful for Gus at my hip.

Fog drifted through the trees and swirled around our feet, softening and obscuring our surroundings, dampening sound, and making the sentient forest feel even more otherworldly.

Once we were out of sight of the academy, Theus halted.

"I would like to translocate us somewhere. Partly to ensure we're away from prying ears. And partly because... well, you'll see."

He seemed to be asking my permission, so I nodded. "All right."

In moments, the haze of a temporary gateway that was the hallmark of the world walkers' power sprang to life. It wasn't one you could see the destination through, which made sense if Theus was worried about being observed.

We stepped through the skin-crawling static together, and suddenly it was daylight and a barren landscape stretched before us.

No. Not barren.

Desolate.

I'd read that even deserts were abundant with their own forms of life. Not so here.

Nothing grew. Nothing moved. And nothing but dust shifted over the vast plain surrounding us. Not so much as a bug. Or a snail for that matter.

In the distance I could see a sagging cottage with no roof, a listing wire fence, and a few dead trees still standing. Beyond that, there was nothing. Even the earth itself was a sickly gray, as if the soil too had been leeched of life. Erosion drew cracks in the land, and the wind picked up that soil as if it weighed nothing, held nothing…

I opened my second sight and confirmed I was not mistaken. Nowhere had I experienced such an utter lack of light. Of life. Of energy. I closed my eyes to be certain I wasn't missing any faint traces, but only sunlight shone through my eyelids.

Wherever we were, the sun had already risen in this part of the world. I estimated it was a few hours from setting, in fact.

"Where are we?" I whispered.

"It was farmland in what used to be known as northern France."

"Used to? What happened?"

But I knew the answer before I'd finished asking.

The Malus.

The air stole from my lungs at the stark reality of that. This was just a tiny speck on the map of the land, the nations, the entire civilizations that the Malus had devoured.

Theus's voice was quiet too. The way people get in the presence of death. Which I supposed was appropriate, because we were standing in a graveyard, in a way. A graveyard the size of a country. A continent.

"This area was devoured by the Malus about forty years ago. It has moved on now that there's nothing left for it to take. In some ways, we are safer here than anywhere else on this planet."

I'd seen pictures of France in an old travel book. Paris, the city of love. Quaint villages nestled within rolling green pastureland or pretty, historic vineyards. Seaside towns clinging to cliffs and hectare upon hectare of sprawling fields planted with lavender or wheat or other food crops or dotted with cattle and wildflowers.

All of it gone now.

"Will it ever grow back?" I asked.

"Yes. In a few hundred years or so, it will. Or significantly less with walker magic and hard work." He hesitated. "My mother brought me here the day she told me I was to become a hollow."

I didn't know how to respond to the revelation about his mother. I placed a hand on his arm and squeezed it. "I'm sorry."

And I was. But the majority of my mind was stuck on *a few hundred years*. I couldn't wrap my head around it. The extent of the devastation.

I'd grown up knowing that at least two-thirds of the old world had been decimated, that it no longer existed, that I'd never see or experience it. But it had never felt more real to me than in that moment.

No wonder the walkers hated the Malus.

This must be all that was left of their entire world. Their *larger* world. How much must they have lost?

I took a deep, shuddery breath.

"Why did you bring me here? What does this have to do with Ellbereth?"

Theus drew in a deep, shuddery breath of his own. For different reasons, I suspected. He'd been here before. Had already known just how devastating the wake of the Malus was.

But from what he'd said, his plan to protect me meant going against the dictates of his own people. At what cost to himself?

He did not answer my questions. Not directly.

"I shouldn't be telling you this. It's forbidden to so much as mention it to an outsider or talk about it among ourselves where someone might overhear." He swallowed, then cracked a half smile. "In fact, I cannot think of a single act I could commit that would make my people more furious."

I didn't smile back. Fear for him gripped my heart. Revealing just how much I'd come to care about this walker. I'd been determined to avoid attachment, and yet... there was something about him that went far deeper than his fathomless green gaze and achingly beautiful face. His steadfastness and unacknowledged strength, his vulnerability, the quiet flashes of humor, his friendship—undeserved.

Despite my best efforts, I knew where every faint freckle lay across the bridge of his nose. Worse, I *didn't* know whether I could still choose to hurt him if it became necessary to succeed in the goals I'd set myself. Because somewhere along the line, he'd become one of the people I wanted to protect.

"Furious enough to kill you?" I asked.

Theus failed to answer that question too.

"Have you ever thought about where life force from the hollows is anchored? It is in a place far away from here, far away from anything really, in a location we believe the Malus will go last of all. We call it something that translates roughly to the Cache of the Last Stand, and it is considered sacred to our people."

I listened in silence, not yet grasping why this topic was so forbidden or what it had to do with me.

"Ellbereth feels free to target you because as a hollow she is protected from your magic. But there is a way to change that. A way that would bind Ellbereth's life force to your own. To irreversibly tie your life with hers."

That sounded like something I distinctly *didn't* want to do. I wanted Ellbereth out of my life, not bound to me forever.

"It is not without risk, and it would require you to travel to the life force cache to do the binding, but it is possible. And it would mean Ellbereth could not kill you without sacrificing herself.

"More than that, by making her well-being dependent on yours, you would effectively tie the hands of her allies too. Including her politically powerful mother who holds sway over half the council. Their relationship is a close one, and I do not believe she would sacrifice her daughter to kill you. Even those who don't feel the same way would at least be given pause by the political ramifications of being responsible for Lady Neryndrith's daughter's death."

"What if Ellbereth *is* prepared to sacrifice herself?"

"She won't. The way she's tried to conceal the attempts on your life is telling. She's not even prepared to lose political face, let alone everything."

Theus's eyes met mine then. "It is the only way I can think of to keep you safe."

I gulped.

"Would it work in reverse? If Ellbereth died in battle or of natural causes or swallowed her own poisonous tongue, would I die with her?"

Theus's shoulders tightened. "Yes." He raked his fingers through his hair and released a breath. "The binding is an ancient but rare ritual. Usually it is performed by lovers who would prefer to die than live without the other, and even then only in the direst of need. Essentially, the binding allows you to draw on one another's life force. So if one half of the pair was afflicted with star sickness—"

"Star sickness?"

"Yes, it's a slow but deadly disease that sometimes afflicts a walker who has traveled too much. We were born to walk across worlds, but traversing through the fabric of the universe is still hard on our bodies. Or so I've heard."

He said the last part under his breath, more to himself than me. But it was a reminder that he would never have the chance to experience world walking for himself. This thing he believed he was born to do. Not even once.

He cleared his throat. "Anyway, if one walker is sick, the binding will allow them both to live relatively normal lives. The healthy partner will be weaker than they would be otherwise of course, but the disease does not cross the bond to their body, and so the lovers can live until old age claims them. If, on the other hand, one of the partners is decapitated for example, they will both die instantly."

Wow. Trying to grasp the repercussions of Ellbereth and I being connected in that way was making me light-headed.

"Given life force and magic are interlinked," I mused, "can the bound pair use each other's magic?"

Theus's lips compressed. "Not usually. But, Nova, this has never been tried with two hollows. Never been tried with a walker and a human. And certainly never tried with someone with your wildcard gift. I don't know what will happen."

I mulled that over, watching Theus's hands clench and unclench in unconscious tension. It seemed unlikely that Ellbereth would gain access to my magic. And if she did? Her fanatical conviction that it was evil would probably ensure she didn't use it.

This path was fraught with danger and a host of ramifications I could barely begin to comprehend. But it was still the best option I had. The *only* one besides give up and die.

So I would take it.

"All right. How do I get to the cache?"

"You can't. It's thousands of miles away and impossible to reach without a gateway."

"Then—"

"I will take you."

I stared at Theus in horror. This walker who had already risked so much, given so much... for me.

Up until this moment, I'd imagined performing the ritual alone. Of keeping Theus entirely separate from the process so any fury would be directed at me. It was for *my* protection after all.

I could claim I'd overheard other kids talking about it and figured it out on my own. Or claim my magic guided me to do it. Anything that would put the onus squarely on my shoulders.

But if the only way for me to get there was with Theus committing an outright act of treason—rather than whispering about it far away from any eavesdroppers—then all chance of him avoiding the fallout was gone.

Even without witnesses, someone was sure to figure out which walker was responsible for transporting me to the life force cache eventually. Our association had not gone unobserved.

Theus, who had only ever been kind to me. Who had been treated so poorly his whole life for something he'd had no control over. Who had overcome all such things to be exceptionally noble and good. Who had already given up half his lifespan and the greatest desire of his heart to become a hollow and fight in the war against the Malus.

"No," I said. My voice was firm, but my stomach sank as my last chance to live slipped through my fingers. "You can't throw away your remaining years for mine. I won't let you."

Theus gazed back, his usually calm demeanor holding an intensity I'd never seen.

"I thought you might say that," he said.

Then he gripped my shoulders and shoved me through another gateway.

CHAPTER THIRTY-FOUR

Stinging, icy wind blasted my face, my body, my hands, making me hyperaware of every inch of exposed skin.

This new landscape was glaringly white as far as the eye could see in every direction. Everything was made of ice. The ground. The distant mountain range. The sluggishly flowing river. Everything but the frozen gray stones jutting up before us.

The frigid temperature and that damned icy wind was threatening to turn me into one more frozen thing to add to this land's collection.

I had never experienced lethal cold in my home settlement in what remained of Los Angeles. I'd grown dangerously chilled after my near drowning, but this? This was worse. The air snatched at my warmth and strength. My face already ached with it, my exposed extremities were turning numb, and I'd been here all of thirty seconds.

I turned my freezing face to the sky. Even that was mostly white. The sun's position had changed again. Hanging low but visible on the horizon and doing nothing to warm us.

Then Theus placed his hand on my arm—a hand he'd used to shove me through his gateway mere moments ago—and heat spread through me.

Not the romantic sort of heat you read about in books. The magically sourced, improving blood flow and preventing hypothermia kind.

"Sorry about pushing you," he said, "but we don't have time to worry about such trivial matters as my life if we want to make it back before breakfast."

I gaped at him. Then shut my mouth before the glacial wind could freeze my tongue to my teeth.

Theus started walking toward one of the towering outcroppings of rock and ice. And since his magical warmth was the difference between life or death—and curiosity was absolutely getting the better of me—I went with him.

The rock loomed larger as we neared, and I noticed this place wasn't lifeless. Not entirely. Some sort of lichen clung to the unforgiving gray stone, and a flicker of motion in the corner of my eye drew my attention to a second thing that wasn't white. There, in the distance, were dark specks, definitely moving. Penguins? Seals? I'd never seen either in real life, and they were too far away to make out, but I knew enough to be certain they weren't polar bears.

I had the growing inkling we were on Antarctica. The faraway frozen continent that no human had ever truly inhabited. A literal half a world away from my family home and who knew how many thousands of miles from France. Or the academy for that matter—wherever it was located.

And I understood why the walkers had chosen this place for their Cache of the Last Stand.

Antarctica was the most barren, the most remote continent they would've found. Too dangerous and too distant for post-invasion human technologies to traverse. And probably the least appealing destination to the Malus who fed on life force.

It wasn't dead, wasn't desolate like that patch of farmland Theus had first taken me to. But it was a lot less tasty than say, the landmass that used to be the United States.

I resisted confirming my suspicion. Theus was breaking enough rules for me. I could let him keep that secret at least.

Ice crunched under our feet, and even with Theus magically warming me, the frigid air in my lungs made the going more difficult than it should've been. It didn't help that I still wasn't a hundred percent after the latest murder attempt.

I was grateful to enter a crevice that I'd failed to spot until we stepped inside. No, not a crevice, a tunnel, leading downward. In any case, the wind could no longer claw at us, and I felt instantly warmer.

We must have been getting close to the cache now. But there were no guards. The location was its own security.

Theus was providing light as well as warmth. The golden luminescence bounced off smooth curves of ice and rock, too perfect to have been carved by anything but magic.

Then we stepped into a grand cavernous chamber of a scale I was utterly unprepared for.

The immense space was yawningly empty, yet every inch of the ice floor, walls, and ceiling were carved with beautiful renderings of landscapes from other worlds, and a warm light emanated from the ice itself to illuminate them.

I suddenly understood why it was forbidden to bring any human here.

Any human, yes. But especially me.

It wasn't the solemn sanctity of the place. The exquisite care to detail that spoke of its sacred significance to the walkers.

It was the staggering, stupendous, blinding amount of life force.

Every hollow in existence had their life energy stored here. And without the barrier of a body or thousands of miles of distance, I instinctively knew that I could drain every single one of them in an instant.

CHAPTER THIRTY-FIVE

"Are you insane?" I hissed at Theus. "Why did you bring me here? I could kill you all, every hollow, right now. Then use that crazy amount of life force to eliminate every walker from the planet!"

Sure the withdrawals would likely kill me afterward, but that wasn't the point.

"I know," Theus said. "But I don't believe you will. And before you decide, there are several things you need to hear."

I gaped at him. Again. For some incomprehensible reason, he trusted me.

Enough that he'd just laid the lives of him and his people in my hands.

He gestured at several seats carved into the wall of ice. These too bore engravings.

"You might as well sit down. This is going to take a while."

The raw, unprotected life force called to my magic. So loudly I could almost hear it. But I shook off the call, the shock, the temptation, the bewilderment, and sat down.

To my second sight, the anchored life energy looked like a forest of glowing golden saplings in the vast, pristine white backdrop of the ice chamber. Beautiful. Overwhelming. And there for the taking.

The bench was warm. Despite that not making any sense in a room carved of frozen water, I was past being surprised by it.

Theus sat beside me.

"There is something about the Malus that the academy will never tell you."

I could see tension in every line of his body, causing the lean musculature across his shoulders and arms to stand out more than usual and sharpening the edges of his cheekbones and jaw. I waited to hear what he had to say.

"We walkers are not the heroes of this story, Nova. Nor are we the villains. Not really. Perhaps, at best, we're the sidekick to both." He paused.

"What do you mean sidekick to both?"

Theus closed his eyes, gathering his resolve perhaps.

"I told you once what it meant to be world walkers. For our entire history up until the Malus, we slipped through the fabric of reality and explored the universe in carefree wonder. Discovering, appreciating, experiencing what each world had to offer. We were carefree, yes, but we ensured we did not upset the complex and fragile balance of those worlds we visited. Despite what you have witnessed, our nature and magic is that of life, and life cannot be sustained without balance.

"One hundred and fifty years ago, a walker slipped into a new world. This world was not like the others. The life there was twisted. The land empty of all but evil. And the evil saw the world walker. It watched as he opened the door back to our world, and some of that evil slipped through with him."

My heart pounded at Theus's words. At the implications. That must mean—

"We are responsible for unleashing the Malus upon the worlds."

Anger surged through me at this matter-of-fact admission, but it was quickly cooled by a level of reluctant understanding. It had been an accident. A horrendous, destructive accident, yes, but how could they have known? How many centuries had they been walking the worlds without incident before one unfortunate happenstance had them stumbling across the Malus world?

I was mad at the walkers. It was undeniable. And yet... I'd learned how easy it was to destroy something simply because you didn't understand it. I well remembered the day I'd come through the runegate and damaged Millicent's wall. Not to mention the lives my magic had taken without my intention.

The walkers had screwed up, it was true. But it was a

mistake that they'd surely paid for a million times over. And they were trying to fix it.

"There's more though," Theus said. And this time when he closed his eyes, he didn't open them again. As if he couldn't bear to look at me.

"When the Malus had devoured our world and we retreated here to yours, we *knew* it would follow. More than that, we wanted it to. It was that or allow it to slaughter every hollow we were forced to leave behind, over half our number, and render us forever homeless. But we came here knowing that it would destroy your planet too—unless we could uncover a new way to fight back."

The knowledge of that reverberated through me like a discordant gong, and all empathy fell away. They had chosen—*knowingly chosen*—to bring about the deaths of billions of people?

My initial burst of anger had been like a flash fire— fast and bright yet fast to fade too. But now the hot embers of rage were building inside me.

How dare they? How dare they sentence so many to death for a tiny hope of their own salvation? Why hadn't they had the grace to lie down and die with the rest of their world?

Oh yes, I had rage aplenty. But there was panic too. They'd failed. We had just ten years left before they'd doomed us all.

Or maybe not *all* of us. Maybe the walkers would

just move onto a new world. To repeat the cycle of destruction all over again.

The wealth of life force shining around me was a reminder that not all the walkers would move on. The hollows at least would suffer the same fate as the rest of us.

Small consolation.

The revelations brought back an old familiar fury. I had come to the academy with the secret goal of learning everything I could about the monsters behind the Agreement that forced human families to give up their firstborn child. To learn about those monsters, then destroy them.

The first three months of life-and-death trials they'd subjected to us hadn't dampened that resolve. I'd gathered each surge of fresh anger and tucked it away along with the old. Weaving them together in a tapestry of purpose and determination, held in abeyance for the right time. Because I'd known, promised myself, the time would eventually come for me to act, and that when it did, I would need to channel every ounce of that anger.

There was so much of it. Anger at the walkers' cold condescension even as they ripped us from our families and forced us to risk our lives without explanation. For the grief and sorrow of those we'd left behind, every family that had been broken, never to be whole again. For the heartbreak and homesickness of knowing I'd been sundered from my father, sister, brother, and mother forever. For the tears on Mila's chubby cheeks as I'd left her on that rooftop. For my brother's fingers clutching my shirt in unspoken anguish. For my own unmet longing for my father's embrace. For the terrifying changes I'd glimpsed in Fletcher that had drained him of the warmth and light that had once defined him. For robbing Ameline of the innocence I'd wanted to preserve. For the terror Bryn must have felt as she lay paralyzed before the shadow stalker in a desperate effort to save her friends. For every casual cruelty. For every life they'd needlessly risked in the ruthless trials and dangerous transformation ritual. And for every seventeen-year-old who would never make it to their eighteenth birthday.

I'd vowed to myself I would avenge them all, that I would tear down the Firstborn Agreement and set these things to rights.

And this was an excellent opportunity to follow through.

Yet I'd learned a great deal since then. Not the least of which was that the walkers demanded their own families give up a child for the fight against the Malus too.

And it occurred to me uneasily that if the walkers had indeed *chosen* to bring the Malus with them, logic suggested they could have left it behind. And if they had *that* ability, they could have instead chosen to dump the devouring darkness on our world and leave us to deal with it alone.

Either way, the threat from the Malus was real. I was convinced of that much.

Which meant killing the hollows would mean wiping out the bulk of the specially trained soldiers who could stand before the Malus without being drained dry. Which in turn would necessitate the sacrifice of even more human lives.

But could I trust what Theus had told me? Could I trust that the walkers' true agenda for the academy and the hollows and the firstborns was what they claimed? That although they had chosen to unleash the Malus on our world, they were now determined to save us?

They'd lied and deceived and hidden so much from us. What else might they have lied about? All the walkers' actions according to the human side of history, even the actions I had witnessed in my short lifetime, had seemed to cause only death and suffering.

Perhaps the best gift I could give humankind was to wipe out the walkers and leave the post-invasion survivors with just one enemy.

And yet... Theus.

He stood as a shining exception to all of that.

I shifted to look at him. He was watching me, patiently waiting for me to process. To react. To ask questions.

He was here, *I* was here, because he was risking his life to save mine. And as furious as I was at walkerkind, Theus hadn't even been born when his people had elected to come to our world, bringing the devastation of the Malus with them.

He was no more guilty of those actions than I was. And his life was worth no less than mine. Yet he was prepared to throw it away. For me.

Could I truly dismiss and reject everything he offered me and repay it with betrayal?

Jeez, my heart and head hurt. I'd been planning, scheming, preparing, fighting for this moment, this opportunity, my entire life. To have the walkers vulnerable before me. To hold the power to right the wrongs and protect the people I loved.

And now that I had it, I wished I didn't.

Because nothing was clear-cut anymore. One of the people I wanted to protect was on the wrong side. And tearing down those I had believed to be our enemies might only lead to more death and pain and destruction.

"Why are you telling me all this?" I demanded of Theus. "Do you *want* me to slaughter you all?"

He had to have known what I could do here. And yet he'd brought me anyway. Why?

And what was I going to do about it?

Despite the suffering he'd undergone at the hands of his family and race, I had never sensed a thirst for vengeance...

Theus reacted as if I'd slapped him. "No. I'm telling you because I trust you. Because I've seen you, Nova. Watched you. Wherever there is a chance to choose life, to choose mercy, you take that option. So long as it doesn't cost the life of someone you're trying to protect.

"You could've killed Ellbereth, killed Healer Invermoore, and every walker there that night they tried to strip you of your magic. Anyone else might have hated them for what they did, but you saw their side. Their heart. And chose to spare them even if it meant they'd come after you again."

That wasn't the whole story. I'd also spared them because I probably would've been executed if I hadn't. Or had that just been my excuse?

"Besides, you have the right to know the full truth before you risk everything to face the Malus."

Theus's observations did not help my indecision. Why was he offering me his life, his trust, his loyalty when even *I* didn't know what was inside me?

My gut writhed with the agonizing conflict of it. Of having the power to choose—truly choose—for the first time in my life and not knowing the right path to take.

Be careful what you wish for.

"But I have still more to tell you," Theus said, "if you're ready to listen?"

I managed a curt nod.

"I know the loss of life is inexcusable, but there was a reason we chose your world, Nova."

My stomach twisted in misery. I wasn't sure I wanted to hear this.

"Lirielle's grandmother had a vision before she died.

A prophecy that foretold salvation would be found here."

I was too dumbfounded to respond. *That* was their big justification? The ramblings of an old woman on her deathbed?

Ramblings that, according to what Cricklewood had said, most of the walkers themselves must place little faith in.

But then Lirielle had predicted my wildcard gift, hadn't she?

"We tried to get around it," Theus continued. "For a hundred years, we tried… But in the end—"

"In the end you slaughtered billions to save your own skins," I snapped. "There is *no* reason that could make that okay!"

Theus bowed his head in concession, but his eyes never left my face.

"I know. But are you so sure you would not do the same? To save your family? Your loved ones? Everything you hold dear?"

My gut twisted with realization and fresh misery. Hell's breath. He had me dead to rights. How could I argue when I was sitting here contemplating wiping out thousands of walkers to do just that?

And I had even less reason to believe the ends would justify the means.

Not that a prophecy was all that great a reason.

Except in a world of magic, where Lirielle had

known about my wildcard gift before it had happened, maybe it was.

I wrestled my seething storm of emotions—rage, guilt, grief, fear, shell shock, and a whole lot more guilt —under a semblance of control. Then asked, "What was the prophecy?"

Theus recited it by heart.

> *Here is the hope that never grew*
> *Here is the dream that never flew*
> *Here is the heart that never beat*
> *This is the sound of worlds' defeat*

> *Wait for the firstborn human witch*
> *Wait for the world walker magic glitch*
> *Wait for the reversal of life and death*
> *Then the nightmare will be laid to rest.*

Theus cleared his throat. "That's a translation of course, but an accurate one."

Ugh. It was so damn vague except for the human and firstborn parts. But the Agreement, the academy, and the walkers' desire for wildcards made a whole lot more sense now.

So long as you were prepared to stake the fate of two worlds on the ramblings of an old woman.

But my conscience twinged again at being so dismissive of Lirielle's grandmother. Lirielle herself was strange and difficult to understand—but strange and difficult to understand didn't mean wrong.

Theus apparently hadn't finished dropping bombshells today.

"Lirielle believes that the firstborn human witch is you." He shifted uncomfortably. "And that I'm the walker with the magic glitch."

Shock and disbelief ricocheted through me.

Theus's green gaze hit me with an intensity that penetrated anyway. There was something in his eyes that I couldn't read, or maybe it was something I didn't want to read.

"I believe Lirielle and her grandmother might be right. Can't you see the balance? The two sides of the coin? Our life magic has wrought so much death. Perhaps your death magic will bring life back to our worlds."

I shook my head in mute negation.

A part of me instinctively rejected the idea that the world would ever make that much sense. But within another part of me, something seemed to resonate, and that was almost as scary as the earnest conviction on Theus's face.

Scrabbling, confused, desperate without grasping the cause, I flung the only thing I could think of back at him.

"If that's true, why are you only telling me this now?"

Theus lifted his chin, like here was one secret he

wasn't ashamed of. "You were already under too much pressure for anyone's sanity. We didn't want to add to it. Besides, knowing wouldn't have altered what you needed to focus on."

He had a point there. Several actually.

"It's as I said before, we walkers are not the heroes of this story. Nor are we the villains, not really. At best, we're the sidekick to both. But, Nova"—his eyes roamed over my face with terrifying hope—"I believe the hero will be you."

More disbelief. Denial. And a tiny tendril of my own awakening hope.

Because standing in this chamber surrounded by the magnitude of life force beyond my prior imaginings, I was beginning to understand just how powerful my wildcard gift could be.

Probably only once. Probably in a way that would result in my body going into shock and death at the withdrawal of that power. But perhaps once was all that would be needed to end the Malus's rampage of destruction.

Despite everything, the vastness of the Malus, the vagueness of the prophecy, the bloody history between humans and walkers that could never truly be put to rights... I was starting to think that maybe, just maybe, my magic *could* be the key to defeating the Malus.

That perhaps the darkness in the circlet had recognized me not because I was unwittingly under its influence, but because in my wildcard power was an enemy worth noticing.

Lirielle's grandmother had predicted someone like me would come. Had believed they would end the nightmare of the Malus. Lirielle believed that person *was* me. And Theus's own conviction was staring me in the face.

Maybe it was time for me to believe too.

I swallowed, noticing my mouth had gone dry.

Theus, still studying me, seemed to realize I was drawing close to a conclusion.

"There is one more thing you should know before you choose what you do within this chamber." He paused.

I waited.

"You have good reason to hate our kind, but if we left now, even if we managed to take the Malus with us, your world would self-destruct. The balance of the atmosphere, oceans, and ecosystems has been pushed far beyond what it can naturally recover from, and it is only our magic maintaining conditions compatible with life. Without walkers, mass extinction would occur across the planet."

That final stunning revelation made all my half-formed plans to one day extract justice from the walkers collapse like a house of cards.

And in its place, I found... acceptance.

Not that what they'd done was okay. It wasn't. It never would be.

And yet I understood why they'd done it. Understood that in some ways, their intentions had been both nobler and more considered than mine.

And that understanding, combined with my relationship with Theus, allowed me to let go of my long-accumulated anger and the prejudices and presumptions that had been caused by it.

I was starting to grasp that while the walkers were not kind, their cruelty came from a difference in the way they saw the world rather than evil intent.

Sure, a lot of them were condescending jerks, but plenty of humans were too. And the walker students I knew were no more responsible for their parents' and grandparents' actions than I was.

Regardless of the past, they were now concerned with saving the species of two worlds. Most humans throughout history were concerned only with saving themselves.

Who really had the higher moral ground?

No. The walkers were not evil. They were not the enemy.

Not anymore.

Maybe they never had been. Not really.

Clinging to anger over past wrongs helped no one. In fact, it might just doom the world.

I stood up, mind made up at last, and a conviction of rightness settled over me like a second cloak.

I had walked into this ice cavern with the weight of fear and desperation, of vengeance and death, of being driven to protect but knowing I was unable to win true freedom or life or safety, pressing heavy on my shoulders.

I would walk out with the weight of the world in their place.

But it was a brighter world. A better world. One with more peace, more liberty, more possibilities than I'd ever dared dream of before.

Because our real enemy was the Malus.

And I'd do everything in my worlds-shaking wild-card power to defeat it.

After that, if I was still alive, I would fight for peace.

CHAPTER THIRTY-SIX

For the first time in a long time, I knew what I had to do.

But before I could do it, the sound of footsteps in the tunnel echoed around the ice chamber.

Theus swallowed and stood, placing himself between me and whoever was coming.

Someone who was about to catch us in the forbidden cache. Where Theus could be killed by his own kind for bringing me.

I stepped past him.

"No," he said. "The world needs you. Let the wrath fall on me."

"According to Lirielle and her grandmother, the world needs you too."

He shrugged. "Perhaps I've already played my part."

I cocked an eyebrow at him. "I just resisted the temptation to rid our planet of pesky walkers, so I'll be damned if I'm going to let anyone get rid of the only pesky walker I'm fond of."

My humor fell away.

"Besides, it's far past time someone stood up for you and recognized your worth. Your family might be blind to it, but I'm not."

He opened his mouth to protest.

"You said you trust me," I reminded him. "So trust me."

The footsteps grew louder.

But I wasn't afraid. A smile tugged at my lips.

Because in this chamber, *I* held the power. And I would use that position of power to broker a deal with whoever was coming. A deal that would keep Theus safe.

CHAPTER THIRTY-SEVEN

The dining hall was almost empty when I stepped inside. Incredibly, we'd arrived early for breakfast.

Well, *I'd* arrived early. Theus—who was still distressed at the debt I'd committed myself to in order to protect him—had gone to his dorm room so we weren't seen walking in together.

It felt like a week had passed.

But instead of the breakfast spread laid out and waiting, I kept seeing the disconcerting memory of my and Ellbereth's life forces converging. Entwining together in an intricate weaving that could never be undone.

I hoped I had not made a terrible mistake.

The bang of a chair crashing to the floor brought me back to the present. The chair must have belonged to Ellbereth because she was storming over with an expression like a thundercloud. There was no sign of the mask of languid civility she usually wore.

The last time I'd seen her had been at the bottom of the arena, politely apologizing about it having to "end this way," just before she'd drowned me.

Now she halted inches from my face and snarled, "What have you done?"

She was so angry that spittle sprayed from her mouth.

No doubt she expected me to fear her, to flinch back.

I stood my ground. And allowed a saccharine smile to spread across my own mouth.

"You might prefer it if we have this conversation in private."

She eyeballed me anew, taking in my relaxed stance, the smile curving my lips, and nodded stiffly. "Fine."

Her minions had risen in her wake, but she waved them back to their seats, and Ellbereth and I found a nice unused room to talk in.

She slammed the door shut and whirled. "What have you done?" she repeated.

I lifted my hand and conjured a bunch of especially thorny roses out of thin air.

Ellbereth's eyes widened as she felt the corresponding drain on her magic. Because it had been *her* magic I'd used.

I smiled apologetically. "I suppose I should've brought you flowers *before* I bound our life forces together the way lovers do. But here." I pushed them into her hands.

She was so shocked she took them.

After the binding had been completed, I'd sensed Ellbereth's life force curled around me. Still separate from my own but ready to draw on if needed.

I'd experimented to see if I could draw not just on her life force, but her magic too. After all, my wildcard gift allowed me to use the magic of snails to ooze slime and the magic of stoneboars to shield myself.

And to my scheming delight, it had worked.

The spellcasting I'd tested my theory with back in the cache had been the smallest tasks I could think of. Lighting the end of my finger. Melting a sliver of ice and then refreezing it.

But here, in front of Ellbereth, I *wanted* her to feel it. To feel the drain as I wielded her power. And because making something from nothing was one of the costliest magics around, the flowers were the perfect illustration of my new ability.

She dropped them to the floor, horror spreading over her angelic face. "How *dare* you?"

I shrugged. "The same way you dared to kill me, I suppose. But you might want to call off your minions now. Because if I die, so do you."

Her face blanched. She must have already guessed, but hearing it confirmed aloud shook her anyway.

I didn't give her time to recover.

"I hear you're descended from a political prodigy, so I'll leave it up to you to decide who else to tell about this. Just remember that your longevity depends on mine. Which I guess makes us kind of allies, if you think about it…"

Ellbereth was shaking her head. "They'll lock you up!"

"Will they? Not everyone fears my magic like you do. Though perhaps they should." I allowed my lips to curve again in a half smile. "But I'd suggest you use your political power to avoid that fate for me too, because if I'm stuck in some cell, I'll have nothing to do but play with your magic."

To drive my point home, I called up the petals strewn over the floor and flung them into the air to float down around us.

"Wouldn't it be a shame if you went from being Ellbereth of Neryndrith, one of the strongest walkers of your year, to a nobody too weak to be remembered?"

If she got any paler, she'd be mistaken for dead.

"What do you want?" she hissed.

"For you to call off your minions, refrain from taking your anger out on any of my friends, and protect my back from any other walkers who think killing me might be a good idea. In return, I'll avoid using your magic except in dire need."

She ground her teeth before answering, searching for a way out. But her only options were to play my game, or go to the authorities and live with the consequences that were liable to be just as painful for her as they were for me. (At least until she'd had time to regroup and devise a new ploy.)

"Fine."

"Glad we could come to an understanding."

I turned my back on her in a deliberate gesture—one that demonstrated my complete lack of fear—and walked out the door.

To the halls I could once again traverse alone. To my friends who would no longer be kidnapped or attacked in their beds. And to breakfast.

Soon we would be divided into our fighting units and sent to the frontline. Where we would meet the nightmare in the light of day.

Soon we would learn the real cost of what I'd done to save my life and then Theus's.

And soon we would find out if the new hope awakened in my chest was based on ramblings or reality. If I was the firstborn destined to defeat the Malus. Or just one of countless others who would die trying.

But for today my friends and I would celebrate the certainty that we'd survive until then.

And for the first time in weeks, I had my appetite back.

Hell, I might even eat more than Griff...

WANT TO LEARN THE STARTLING
SECRET GUS WILL NEVER SHARE
WITH NOVA?

READ THIS FUN AND FAST BONUS
SCENE AND FIND OUT!

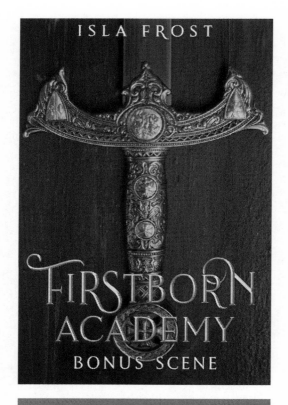

READY FOR THE EPIC CONCLUSION TO
NOVA'S STORY?

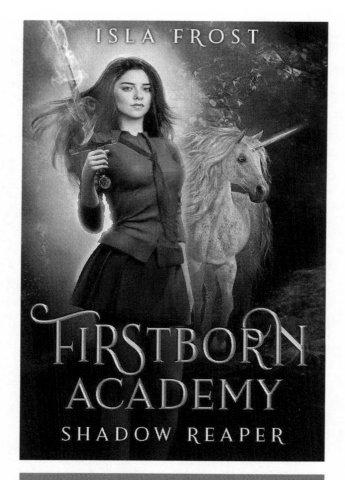

ABOUT THE AUTHOR

Isla Frost is the pen name of a bestselling mystery author whose first love has always been fantasy. She loves to write about strong heroines in fast-paced stories full of danger, magic, and adventure that leave you feeling warm and satisfied.

She also loves apple pie.

For sneaky discounts on new releases and occasional bonus content, sign up at www.islafrost.com

Made in the USA
Middletown, DE
07 January 2020